W9-ABS-829

Straight

Straight

Steve Knickmeyer

Random House: New York

 Published in the United States by Random House, Inc., New York, and simultaneously in Canada by Random House of Canada Limited, Toronto.

Library of Congress Cataloging in Publication Data
Knickmeyer, Steve, 1944–
Straight.
I. Title.
PZ4.K6914St [PS3561.N425] 813′.5′4 75–40017
ISBN 0–394–40190–5

Manufactured in the United States of America
9 8 7 6 5 4 3 2

First Edition

for my wife Linda
who gets the last laugh

Straight

Prologue

"State your name and occupation, please."

"Steve Cranmer. I'm a private investigator."

"You conduct your business here in Oklahoma City?"

"That's correct."

"For how long?"

"Approximately eighteen months."

"And before that?"

"I worked in the same capacity for the government."

"Could you be a little more specific, please?"

"It's classified information."

The defense attorney's chair squeaked as he pushed it away from the counsel table and rose to his feet. He was a small man with a prominent nose, dressed in an immaculate blue suit. The attorney, Ronald Haring, made a grand gesture and smiled winningly at the jury. "We'll stipulate Mr. Cranmer's qualifications, your Honor," he said.

Judge East said in a bored tone, "Let the record so show."

Assistant District Attorney Paul Windfield, who was questioning Cranmer, bowed graciously to Haring and continued: "Now, Mr. Cranmer, I noticed you are dependent upon a cane for walking. Is it true you were injured while serving your country?"

Haring stood quickly and protested: "Objection, your Honor! That is hardly . . ."

"Objection sustained. Mr. Windfield, I'm sure you realize Mr. Cranmer's health is irrelevant to this case."

Windfield shrugged. "Not entirely, your Honor. But I'll move along." He gave the jury a long-suffering look. "All right, Mr. Cranmer, do you recall your whereabouts on July 3 of this year?"

Cranmer shifted uncomfortably in the witness box, trying to find a less cramped position. "Yes," he said disinterestedly.

"And where were you at approximately nine-thirty P.M. on that date?" Windfield prompted.

"Blue's Booze."

"And that is . . . ?"

"A liquor store at 45th and May."

"That's near your office?"

"Right. I'm in the Trinity Building."

"Fine. Now, did anything unusual happen while you were in the liquor establishment?"

Cranmer's smile was a partial sneer. "Yes."

Windfield looked expectantly at Cranmer, then, when it became apparent Cranmer wasn't going to expand upon his answer, asked, "Could you relate to the jury what occurred?"

"The store was robbed."

"You were inside the store during the robbery?"

"That's correct."

"Could you give the details of the robbery?"

Cranmer sighed. "A man walked into the store with a brown paper sack in his hand. He went to the cash register. Tony Blue, the proprietor of the store, was sitting on a stool behind the cash register. The man pulled a pistol, a .38-caliber Smith and Wesson revolver, aimed it at Tony Blue and demanded the money in the cash register. Tony put the money in the man's paper bag, and the man left."

"Do you remember the robber's exact words?"

"He said, 'Put the bread in the bag, Mac. Don't play no games and won't nobody get hurt. I'm serious about this.' "

"That's all he said?"

"It was enough. He made his point."

A few members of the jury smiled. Windfield smiled with them, trying to form an alliance.

"Fine. Now, if you'd give a few more details about your role, Mr. Cranmer. Exactly where were you when the robbery occurred?"

"By the bourbon."

Laughter rippled through the courtroom, and Judge East reached for his gavel. But the merriment died before the judge had to still it.

"And where is the bourbon located?" Windfield asked patiently.

"About six feet from the cash register."

"So you had a good view of the robber?"

"That's correct."

"Was he masked?"

"No mask."

"What was he wearing?"

Cranmer shifted position again and scratched his nose. "Green army fatigue jacket, white turtleneck, blue jeans, boots."

"And you had a clear view of this man?"

"Yes."

"Do you see the man in this courtroom now?"

"Yes."

"Would you point him out to the jury, please?"

Cranmer negligently pointed a finger at the defendant, a swarthy white man sitting next to Ronald Haring. Veins protruded in the man's neck, and his eyes were bloodshot.

"May the record show Mr. Cranmer identifies the defendant?" Windfield said.

Judge East cleared his throat and announced: "Let the record so indicate."

"Now, Mr. Cranmer," Windfield said portentously. "Would you close your eyes, please, and keep them shut until I tell you to open them?"

Cranmer sighed and closed his eyes. Haring pushed his chair away from the counsel table but did not rise.

Windfield said, "Now, Mr. Cranmer, is it true your profession demands keen observation?"

"Yes."

"As I said in my opening argument, eyewitnesses do not normally provide the most valid testimony. But you have been trained through a long career as an investigator—qualifications which even the defense has recognized—to observe accurately and recall that which you observed. Would you say that's a fair statement, Mr. Cranmer?"

"Yes."

"Fine. Now, are you acquainted with the attorney for the defense, Mr. Haring?"

"I am."

"Well, he won't do, then." Windfield winked at the jury. "Are you acquainted with any members of the jury?"

"No."

"Fine. Now, if I speak of the man in the jury box who is sitting the closest to you—Mr. Beck, that is—just to your right, would you know to whom I was referring?"

"Yes."

"Fine. Now, Mr. Cranmer, I'm going to ask you to give us a description of that juror, Mr. Beck. Since you are unacquainted with him, your description will be based solely on the observation you have made today, is that correct?"

"All right."

"And I'd like to point out that since the rule has been invoked in this trial and witnesses are not allowed in the courtroom, you have only been able to observe the juror for the length of time you've been on the witness stand."

Cranmer remained silent.

Haring sprang to his feet. "I object, your Honor! This is a grandstand trick to influence the jury, and I . . ."

Windfield interrupted him. "I'm simply attempting to support the reliability of Mr. Cranmer's testimony . . . No, keep your eyes closed, Mr. Cranmer. Your Honor, Mr. Cranmer's identification is an important part of our case, and I think the jury deserves to see how reliable that testimony is."

Judge East's own curiosity was evident in his eyes. "I'll overrule the objection," he said. "The demonstration seems relevant to me."

"Exception," snapped Haring.

"Granted," said the judge dryly. "Proceed, Mr. Windfield."

"Thank you, your Honor. Would you describe the juror, Mr. Cranmer?"

The jury watched Cranmer expectantly. Haring remained on his feet, glaring.

Cranmer recited impassively: "He's about thirty. I haven't seen him standing, so I can't be positive about his height, but judging from his sitting position he'd be about five feet ten, unless he has unusually long or short legs. Weight: about a hundred and sixty. Black hair, parted on the left side, medium length, covering most, but not all, of his ears. Eyes: hazel or brown. Bushy eyebrows. No sideburns, unless they're concealed by his hair. Standard nose, small cleft in chin. Wearing a green suit with a blue tie that doesn't match. Tie tack rather than clasp. Wears watch on the right wrist. Bites his nails. What else? Sallow complexion. I can't see his shoes. No visible scars."

Mr. Beck, the juror, looked at his fingernails self-consciously, and a murmur of astonishment ran through the jury. Cranmer's description had been accurate in every detail.

"That's fine, Mr. Cranmer," Windfield said preeningly. "You may open your eyes now. I have no further questions."

Cranmer opened his eyes, glanced at the juror as if checking out his memory, then turned his gaze to Ronald Haring. His knee was throbbing. He hoped Haring would be brief, so he could get off the stand and take a couple of pain pills.

Haring attacked instantly. "How much had you had to drink the night you were in the liquor store?"

"A few drinks."

"And you went to Blue's Booze to replenish your supply of liquor?"

"I believe that's the function of liquor stores."

"Just answer my questions, Mr. Cranmer, if you please. Were you drunk on the night of July 3?"

"No."

"But you'd had a few drinks?"

"Yes."

"As an expert investigator, are you aware of the effect of a single ounce of alcohol on a man's perception?"

"Yes."

"Yet you expect this jury to believe your perception was unimpaired?"

"Sure," Cranmer said carelessly.

Haring snorted. "Don't you think," he said, spacing his words for emphasis, "that your grandiose display of memory and observation in describing Mr. Beck might have failed if you had impaired your perceptions with a few drinks before attempting it?"

Amusement glinted in Cranmer's eyes. He paused, allowing a tense silence to build in the courtroom. Haring hunched his shoulders and glared at Cranmer. Windfield doodled on a yellow legal pad. The defendant's veins bulged.

Finally Cranmer said expressionlessly, "I don't think that's valid."

"And why not?"

"I had four drinks with lunch."

This time Judge East had to use his gavel to quiet the courtroom. The D.A. smiled benignly at the jury. Haring recovered quickly, but he was unable to shake Cranmer's aplomb in thirty minutes of cross-examination.

The court recessed for fifteen minutes following Cranmer's testimony. Cranmer picked up his cane, levered himself out of the witness stand and limped over to the prosecution's table. He chatted briefly with Paul Windfield.

"Pretty good trick," Cranmer said.

Windfield chuckled. "Yep. It's nice to see Ron get flustered. He even forgot to ask if I'd coached you to watch that juror carefully."

Butch Maneri left his pew in the audience, walked over to Cranmer and patted him on the shoulder.

"Way to fire, dad," he said. "You done good."

Maneri, a slim, well-muscled redhead, had come to Oklahoma City several months before to team with Cranmer. They had met in a town called Two Kettle, where they had formed an odd kinship powerful enough to overcome the fact that Cranmer had proved Maneri's sister a killer. After the trial and Cranmer's flat, dispassionate and damning testimony, Maneri had escorted his sister to jail and migrated to the City. Maneri held a position somewhere between partner and assistant: more than an assistant but less than a partner. Cranmer would have welcomed a partnership, but Maneri was afraid of the chains.

Cranmer said, "Let's go impair our perceptions, young Maneri."

"Aren't you going to stick around to see what the jury does?" Windfield protested. "We've only got the instructions and the closing arguments left. Haring won't dare put that clown on the stand."

"My being here won't change the verdict," said Cranmer.

Windfield shook his head. "Well, you locked him up pretty tight, Steve. Thanks."

"Sure," Cranmer said. "I'm always here to serve."

He and Maneri left the courtroom. In the corridor Cranmer approached a water fountain. He extracted a medicine bottle from his coat pocket, removed two round yellow tablets, inserted them in his mouth, bent over and filled his mouth with water, then jerked his head back and swallowed water and pills.

Maneri watched with amusement. "Man, you sure make a production out of it," he commented.

"I've got a weak throat," said Cranmer. "Christ, you'd think they'd make that witness box big enough for a full-grown man."

"They don't want their witnesses falling asleep," said Maneri. "We'll have to make that drink a quickie. I've got to hit Tinker at four, pick up Gail and head for Dallas."

Cranmer grinned at him. "You sure you're up to a Texas-OU weekend? Your stomach may not last."

"Oh, it hasn't bothered me too much lately. Anyway, I need a handicap to match your knee. That way you can't be the only martyr in the office."

"Terrific," muttered Cranmer. His knee was a constant reminder of the theorem that when a knee meets an explosive bullet, the flesh and bone will always lose. He owed his departure from the classified government agency to a huge Japanese named Po who had an affinity for mercury-tipped bullets.

Cranmer spotted a weight/fortune machine in the hall of the courthouse. "I'd better see if my ordeal on the stand cost me any weight," he said. He climbed onto the scale, stuck a penny in the slot and watched the spinning dial.

The machine told him he weighed 174 pounds and was going to take a trip.

Cranmer made a face at the machine. "Everyone who weighs between one-sixty and one-eighty is going on a journey," he sneered. "This contraption must be thinking about you going to Dallas; I'm planning to stay home and watch the tube."

"You never can tell, dad," said Maneri. "That's the joy of life."

"Yeah," Cranmer said dourly. "Let's get that drink."

They left the courthouse, Maneri slowing his pace to match Cranmer's limp.

In their wake, a hefty woman stepped onto the weighing machine.

The dial spun and the fortune changed.

One

Richard Straight didn't count his first two kills. They had been legitimate, for at the time he had been one of New York City's Finest. The first man Straight had killed was a burglar. The newspapers had described him as Brown Dawson, forty-three, of no certain address. He had been a white man with a scraggly beard, grown not for chic but because he couldn't afford a razor or blades. Straight and his partner had seen the man inside a drugstore brandishing a pistol at the frightened owner. They had been on a regular patrol.

Straight entered the drugstore with his Police Special in his hand. He said "Freeze, mister" in a voice that quivered. The burglar spun around to face the unexpected threat, and Straight shot him four times.

Number one.

The standard police inquiry cleared Straight of any malfeasance. But the glow Straight felt worried him. He went home every day after his shift and read Camus and Sartre for a solid month after the kill.

His wife, Jill, cried in the bathroom late at night. For Straight not only had no sexual desire, he had no inclination to speak to his wife or even to admit her existence.

While sitting in the living room wearing his uniform, he would listen to Tchaikovsky's *Pathétique* for hours on end. He read on the album cover of the symphony that Tchaikovsky had died nine days after the first performance of the *Pathétique*. The composer had made the error of drinking a glass of unboiled water, which the album cover called "a foolish mistake in the face of the cholera epidemic raging in Russia." For several nights Straight boiled a glass of water and sipped it while listening to the music.

Straight came out of his shell two months after the kill. There was no particular reason for his emergence. But a healthy, energetic young man cannot spend all his time examining his soul. He returned home from work one day and his greeting peck for Jill turned into a searching kiss. Straight rediscovered sex. Jill went into the bathroom afterward and cried. But these tears were warm, for she had her man back.

Three years later Straight chalked up his second kill. This one was a Puerto Rican youth wielding a knife. The boy's name was Ramirez. He had carved his girl friend up and had similar ideas about Straight. This time Straight wasn't nervous. He shot the Puerto Rican twice, and he didn't fire the second shot until he had gauged the effect of the first.

Straight was a detective now, so he had killed one man while wearing a uniform and one man while wearing a suit. He enjoyed killing the Puerto Rican. He stood over the body, smiling, and felt a quiet urge to take the boy's knife and stab him with it. But he by-passed the pleasure.

The review board gave Straight a commendation for his second kill.

He listened to Tchaikovsky again that night, but this time he sipped a whiskey sour and had a twinkle in his eye. After the symphony and two drinks were completed, Straight took Jill out and bought her a steak.

Straight was transferred to the homicide division and worked there happily for two years. He got to see a lot of bodies and he solved several killings. His captain decided Straight had a knack for analyzing murder.

Straight was now reading Kant with dedication. It was a struggle, but he felt it increased his knowledge and perception of the life process. Since he had accepted death as an integral part of life, any progress he made in understanding life was also progress in comprehending death.

He had developed a good reputation throughout New York

City. People spoke of him as a straight shooter. He enjoyed both the pun and the actuality. He had discovered that investigation and vengeance gave him the same glow as killing a man. He didn't realize his first kill had dictated the remainder of his life, until his wife was murdered.

He had been tracking a professional hit. A newspaper reporter had been wasted. The man had written several complimentary stories about Straight, and Straight was reveling in a righteous investigation.

Straight identified the button man as an import from Chicago. He went to that city, worked over the button man and learned who had employed him. Then he returned to New York City and walked into the middle of the mob. Straight was sure the syndicate would be afraid to roust a cop, and he started applying pressure.

He paid a heavy price for his misconception. The bomb in the car had been meant for him, but it spread Jill over the garage.

Straight started boiling water again. His captain refused to let him continue the investigation. It was the first time Straight had realized the strength of the mob.

He was a realist. Jill was gone, and he could see no percentage in joining her. So he went to see the man who had hired the button man from Chicago. His name was August McEachern and he lived in a remote, spacious house in Oyster Bay.

Straight offered his services. McEachern was suspicious, but Straight wasn't the first man he had bent.

The first job was a test, and it resulted in the kill Straight counted as number one. It was a simple hit in New Orleans. Straight did the killing, and an old hand went along to keep tabs on him. Straight walked into a crowded restaurant and shot a man who had been embezzling prostitution profits. He shot the man one time in the head, dispassionately, and in the midst of all the confusion, casually walked out of the restaurant. McEachern gave him $5,000.

In the following years Straight handled eleven more jobs for McEachern. He was soon a trusted employee, and McEachern began to call on him to use his homicidal talents in more sensitive jobs.

Straight developed a new reputation. It wasn't as widely

recognized as his reputation as a good cop had been, but it was more potent. The mention of Straight's name could strike fear into the hearts of a handful of men throughout the United States. He became an expert in accidental death.

His last seven kills had been written off as accidents. And Straight's fee had increased to $20,000 per job. He now lived in a small house in Syosset and worked no more than twice a year.

He invested his profits in records and books. He drank good whiskey. He had no friends. He hadn't slept with a woman in six years. He thought of himself as content.

Straight was reading Spinoza and listening to Mozart, when he was interrupted by the telephone. He picked it up and said, "Yes." The phone rarely rang, so it was somewhat of an occasion.

"Hello, Richard," murmured a gravelly voice.

Straight waited.

"I have another task for you," said August McEachern.

Straight said nothing.

McEachern gave a rumbling laugh. "Ah, you're an amiable person, Richard," he said. "Do you need to get pencil and paper?"

"I'll remember it," Straight said.

"All right. The man's name is Arthur Taber. He runs a jewelry store in Solano, Oklahoma. It's an outside contract, and we want it to look like suicide."

"Jesus bleeding Christ," Straight complained. "Oklahoma?"

"It should be warmer there," said McEachern. "Solano is a little dump, about three thousand people. You shouldn't have any trouble finding your way around."

"Yeah, and all three thousand people will know I'm there," Straight said. "These villages are murder."

"Well, that's your problem, isn't it?" McEachern said.

He gave Straight some names and addresses. Straight gazed blankly at the paper on his wall.

"One more thing, Richard," said McEachern. "I'm going to send a man with you. A trainee, so to speak."

"Just a minute," Straight said. He set the receiver down

crossways on the telephone and stood motionless for a moment listening to the music.

It sounded wrong. His was a one-man vocation and McEachern knew it.

He picked up the phone again. "I'd rather work alone," he said.

"I'm not giving you a choice, Richard," McEachern said smoothly. Any threat in his voice was understated. "You're the best accident man I have. I expect you to share your experience."

Straight knew better than to voice another complaint. "Who is it?" he asked resignedly.

"A man named Coady. I'm sending him mostly as an observer, you understand. You are to do the actual kill, but I want him to be in on the planning. I know he can hit people. I want him to learn how to manage it with grace, with flair. I'll have him meet you in Oklahoma City. You'll have to fly there and then rent a car to get to Solano."

"How will I know him?" Straight asked.

"What name will you use?"

"Spinoza," Straight said. "Oscar Spinoza."

"You'll be paged," said McEachern.

"All right. Any time limit?"

"Just make sure of it."

"Do I get anything extra for hauling this Coady along?"

"Now, Richard." McEachern laughed. "By rights, you shouldn't get as much. After all, you'll have somebody to split the work with."

Straight grimaced. "Twenty thousand plus expenses?"

"All right. Leave tomorrow."

Straight replaced the receiver, sighed, lifted it again and called American Airlines. He made a reservation for the next day under the name of Oscar Spinoza.

He had never been to Oklahoma. He wished it could stay that way.

Hamilton Coady spent most of his time at Pat's Pool Hall in Sacramento. He liked to watch people shoot pool. Pat's also had a card table, and there was usually a draw poker game going on. Coady liked to watch the poker games. He was not a gambler, but he got a vicarious thrill from watching other people play. He had learned long ago he was not clever enough to gamble successfully.

The phone call came at 3:18 P.M.

"Coady?"

"Right."

"Be home at six. We've got a job for you."

"Yes, sir. Thanks." Coady hung up and grinned.

He ambled back over to the card table and watched a few more hands. Then he headed for his apartment, in case they arrived early.

Coady was large. His six-two frame supported 250 pounds. His clothes fit him poorly. His nose had been broken several times and was spread across the center of his face like melted chocolate. His hands were huge, blunt objects. Coady made his living with them. His favorite movie was *The Boston Strangler.*

Rimson appeared at Coady's apartment exactly at six o'clock. He was a slender man who wore tailored suits. Rimson and Coady sat at the kitchen table, and the slender man started giving instructions. He wrote the information down for Coady.

"You're going to meet a man named Spinoza in Oklahoma City tomorrow," Rimson said. "He's a hit man. You're going to do a job with him. He'll be in charge, and you'll follow directions. But after he hits the Oklahoman, we want you to hit him. Hit him and lose the body. Understand?"

"Sure." Coady grinned.

"It's worth five thousand dollars," said Rimson. "Page him at the airport and let him take it from there. Just make sure you finish it."

Rimson gave Coady a plane ticket, wrote down Coady's flight time and Spinoza's flight time and left the apartment.

Coady got a beer out of his refrigerator. He downed half the beer in a single swallow, then cracked his knuckles for a while. He turned on the television, but there was nothing on except news, so he turned it off again. He finished his beer and crumpled the can.

. . .

Will Rogers World Airport surprised Straight. He hadn't really thought Oklahomans moved about in stagecoaches, still, the modern contours of the Oklahoma City airport didn't match his preconceptions.

Straight went upstairs to the bar and paid $2.50 for a whiskey sour. It wasn't worth it, but it was wet. A song about a dead skunk reverberated from the juke box. Straight listened to it unbelievingly.

The page came over the speaker as Straight finished off his drink. He popped the cherry in his mouth and went in search of the information booth.

A young girl with long blond hair motioned him to a telephone. He picked it up and said, "Yes," into it.

"Spinoza?"

"That's who."

"This is Coady."

"Where are you?" Straight asked.

"In the phone booth behind you."

Straight looked behind him. Three men were using telephones. The one who looked like an overworked boxer flashed him a grotesque wink.

"Well, come on out, for Christ's sake," Straight said. "You're not on Candid Camera."

"Oh. All right."

Coady hung up the phone and walked over to Straight. The men looked each other over without shaking hands. Jesus, Straight thought, this guy probably moves his lips when he watches television.

"They say I'm supposed to do what you say," Coady said.

Straight nodded and scratched his cheek. "Let's get a car," he said.

They went to the Hertz counter. Straight showed the girl his Spinoza driver's license and rented an LTD.

"Wouldn't it be smarter to use a phony name?" Coady asked when they were on the road.

Straight looked at him thoughtfully, then said, "No, it's too much trouble to get the documents. Nobody's going to tie this car to the job."

"But what if they do?" Coady persisted.

"If I mess it up that bad, I'm dead anyway," said Straight.
Coady silently agreed with the last part of his statement.

Straight examined the map and whistled scornfully. "Ham," he said, "would you believe we're heading for a county with a total population of five thousand?"

"Yeh, I'll believe almost anything," said Coady.

"Solano's the county seat, it says here. Must be a thriving burg."

"San Diego's got a lot more people," said Coady.

Straight looked at him blankly, failing to see a connection.

"I hit a guy in San Diego once," Coady explained. "At that big zoo. Jesus, it was lovely. He was kind of an old dude, and he was watching the monkeys. They got a little rail there you can lean on and watch the monkeys. So I mosey up and stand beside this dude at the rail. We watch the monkeys for a while. Then when the crowd thins out some I reach over and put my arm around the guy's shoulders. He don't jump over a couple of feet. He probably figures I'm some kind of queer. Then I slip my hand around his throat, right there in the middle of the zoo with the monkeys watching. I get his windpipe."

Coady flexed the loglike fingers of his right hand. "It takes seven seconds to kill a dude with that hold. I count to ten squeezing to make sure. Then I brace the guy up on the rail and wander off. He looks like he's still watching the monkeys, except his legs are bent kind of funny.

"Jesus, I almost come in my pants. I mean, you know, it was lovely to waste the dude right there in the middle of a crowd and not have nobody know what the hell's going on. I mean to tell you I partied that night. Got me two broads and made them do everything you can think of. And I only had to clobber one of them."

Coady smiled at Straight. Straight folded the road map and put it on the dash, then wheeled the Ford back onto the road.

"Looks like the closest town of any size to Solano is Medwick," he said. "We'll headquarter there."

Coady turned on the television in the hotel room and dug a pint of Cutty Sark out of his suitcase.

Straight unpacked, hanging his clothes carefully in a doorless closet. He put a holstered .45 Colt in a rickety chest of drawers.

Coady peered at the gun. "That what you gonna use?" he asked.

Straight gave a brief negative shake of his head. "This is supposed to be a suicide, right? It weakens a suicide theory if the victim is hit with a foreign weapon. I'll have to improvise."

Coady nodded and popped his knuckles. "You been around some, huh?" he said. "How many jobs you done?"

Straight shrugged.

Coady looked at the television but spoke to Straight. "I wasted seven guys," he said. "All over the country. One of the guys turned out to be a woman. But nobody's ever got a sniff of me. Where you operate out of, Spinoza?"

"Newport News, Virginia," Straight said.

"Never heard of it. What's there?"

"Not much. There's an army base, Fort Eustis, otherwise known as Fort Useless. Lot of transient military around, so it's a pretty good place to remain undetected."

Coady grunted. "I'm in Sacramento," he said.

Straight nodded disinterestedly, slipped off his suit jacket and settled down with a volume of Kierkegaard.

Coady sucked Scotch and said, "Hey, did you hear the one about the Baptist preacher?"

Straight sighed and shook his head.

"Well, there was this Baptist preacher," Coady said. "Kind of a young guy, you know. So one day a new choir director comes to work at his church. She's a young-looking box. Tits out to here. Now this preacher's going around with a hard-on inside his smock all the time. So one day he builds up his courage, you know, and asks this broad how about it. She says, 'Hell, I've just been waiting for you to ask.' So they go down in the basement and this broad pulls off her clothes and her tits are sticking out like, you know, watermelons. The old preacher grabs one in each hand and goes to work. But there ain't no place to lay down in the basement. He don't know what to do, but she says, 'Hell, Charlie, let's do it standing up.' She pulls up his smock and climbs on. They're fucking like whales standing there, and this preacher says, 'Goodness, I hope none of the congregation walks in. They might think we was dancing.' "

Coady roared. Straight smiled.

"Get it?" said Coady. "Them Baptists might think they was dancing."

Straight nodded. "I only remember one joke," he said. "It takes place in the Old West, where the law of the gun prevailed. Two gunfighters have an argument. One of them sets out for revenge. He rides out to where the other gunfighter has a ranch. First he burns down the barn. Then he goes into the main house. He finds the gunfighter's wife and baby. He rips all the clothes off the woman, then while she's standing there naked, he kills the baby. Next he rapes the woman. He spends the afternoon there, raping the woman. Then he pistol-whips her and leaves her to die.

"Before the woman dies her husband shows up. He sees the ashes of the barn, his dead baby and his dying wife. He cradles her head tenderly in his arms and asks her who did it. She tells him, and then she dies.

"The victim rides into town and finds the other gunfighter in the saloon. He walks up to him and says, 'Are you the one who burned my barn?'

" 'That's right,' says the gunfighter, cool as ice.

" 'Did you kill my little baby?' he says with tears in his eyes.

" 'I killed the kid.'

" 'Did you rape my wife all afternoon and then kill her?'

" 'I did it and I enjoyed it.'

"Then the victim leans up real close to the gunfighter, stares him right in the eye and says, 'Well, listen, buddy, you'd better cut that shit out.' "

Coady looked at Straight in puzzlement. Straight chuckled and resumed reading.

Straight parked the rented Ford at an angle in front of the dilapidated Solano County Courthouse. Immediately south of the courthouse was Taber's Jewelry, sandwiched between a tavern and a barbershop. There was enough traffic around the courthouse to keep Straight and Coady from being conspicuous.

"Get us a newspaper," Straight ordered.

Coady got out of the car and bought a newspaper from a rack in front of the courthouse. Straight started reading the *Medwick Herald.* Coady watched the jewelry store.

"Say, our man's in the paper," said Straight. "I think this article might tell us why he's supposed to be hit."

"You mean you don't know?" Coady asked skeptically.

"I never ask," said Straight. "Here, read this."

The article appeared under the byline of Donald Dorne:

SOLANO GRANT IN TROUBLE

The small town of Solano, southwest of Medwick, may pull a first on the federal government. In these days of revenue sharing and federal grants, most areas have their hands out.

But Solano is considering handing over $200,000 back to the government. The money was received in August from the Economic Development Administration (EDA) for the construction of a new courthouse complex in Solano.

Before accepting the grant, the Solano city council, headed by Mayor Peter Brindle, checked with three local merchants to insure they would be willing to sell their property to the City if the grant money became available.

The merchants, jeweler Arthur Taber, tavern operator Sam Archer and barber Anthony Tomas, all let their property be appraised and, according to Brindle, promised to sell.

"The problem now is with Taber," said the mayor. "He claims all he signed was an agreement to the accuracy of the appraisal. Now he wants more money. Coupled with this is the problem of inflation and labor. We just can't be sure the $200,000 will cover the cost of the proposed construction."

Archer and Tomas both told the *Herald* they wanted to sell their property.

But Taber says he was misled. "I made no promises," stated the jeweler. "I'm not ready to retire yet. The price I've been offered would be fair if all I wanted to do was sell the building and get out of business. But I would want to relocate, and their offer gives me nothing for moving expenses. I figure it would take a minimum of $20,000 for me to move into another building and secure it. After all, I must protect precious gems. I can't operate out of an old barn."

Michael Rope, Taber's partner in the jewelry store, who also signed the evaluation listing, could not be reached for comment.

Norman architect, Jeremiah Kilduff, who had already designed Solano's new courthouse complex, said, "This is a typical holdup by a small-town egotist. Taber is trying to make a killing."

Brindle said if Taber's property can't be gained at the original price, the project will be junked. "We can't afford to support Taber for the rest of his life," stated the mayor.

The plans for the new building call for a combination courthouse/city hall.

Brindle said the city council would make a decision at its Tuesday night meeting as to whether or not the EDA grant will be trenured in a sweeping violet bridal EDA grant will be returned.

Solano may lose its new building, but there's a chance the government will reward them with a medal for economy.

"This Taber character don't seem any too popular," Coady decided.

"Let's go check his house," Straight said.

It was time for a dry run.

Straight parked two houses down from Taber's. Observation and discreet inquiry had revealed the house would be empty at this time. Taber was at the jewelry store, and his wife, Denise, was on a shopping trip to Oklahoma City. The man who had told Straight about the shopping expedition had leered when he mentioned it—so perhaps she did more than shop. All that interested Straight was the fact she was gone.

Straight left Coady in the car as a lookout. Coady was to watch for mailmen, garbagemen, anyone whose comings and goings might have a pattern to them. If anyone approached the Taber house, he was to honk three times. There was a back door through which Straight could disappear.

The Taber house consisted of two stories. The first level was brick, the second, wood. The brick was yellow; the wood, white. The house was set back from the street about fifty feet. The lawn was still green and neatly trimmed although it was October. Either Taber had a gardener or he spent a lot of time in the yard.

Straight adjusted his tie and walked to the front door with

assurance. There was no answer to his knock, so he removed a small rectangle of hard celluloid from his suit jacket and forced the lock. No difficulty. He checked the doorframe to insure he had left no marks and went into the house.

On the first floor were a kitchen, dining room, living room, den and study. All the rooms were large. Expensive furniture was scattered sparingly about the house. The carpet was thick and the drapes plush. Straight spent five minutes gazing at the book titles in the study. It was a Book-of-the-Month Club variety. He snorted and went to the desk.

All the drawers opened save one. He glanced in each drawer, then slipped out a straight piece of metal and fiddled the locked drawer open. It contained a black address book. Straight relaxed in the chair behind the desk and skimmed through the book. He recognized no names. He wondered what there was about the address book that made it worth locking up.

He started to go upstairs, but it occurred to him there ought to be a bathroom on the first floor. He found a sliding door in the den next to the fireplace which led to a small bath. The first-floor bath held no personal effects.

The second level of the house was bedrooms. Straight found what he was searching for in the large upstairs bathroom. A straight razor in a black leather case. Straight removed it and tested its sharpness against the hair on his forearm. He made a face at himself in the mirror. The thought of using a straight razor appealed to him. The nomenclature was appropriate.

Straight went through the bedrooms without finding a weapon of any sort, then he left the house. He had relocked the desk drawer, and he locked the front door behind him. No signs of his entry were apparent.

Coady said nobody had showed. They drove back to Medwick.

Coady uncorked another pint of Cutty Sark. "Hey, Spinoza," he said, "you ever been to New Orleans?"

Straight finished a paragraph in the book he was reading, and shook his head. "Why?" he asked.

"Well, I was just thinking about this one time I went there to hit a guy," said Coady. "He spent a lot of time down there in the

French Quarter, in that big bar that goes round and round and you can look out at the water."

"A big bar that goes round and round," said Straight.

"Right. No shit, you don't even have to be drunk to fall down. Thing spins around real slow. It's up on top of a big hotel or office building or something, I forget. Anyways, at night they got a parking lot that's practically empty. The bar can be full, and the parking lot will still be empty. I think most of the people probably walk over there from Bourbon Street or something.

"So I sit in this bar going round and round three nights, watching this dude. Each night I follow him out and some motherfucker's using up space in the parking lot and I have to let him go.

"Finally, on the fourth night I follow him out and the parking lot's empty as advertised," Coady said. "I walk up to the target and ask him where in the hell Al Hirt's place is. He turns around to show me and I grab him with the old seven-second hold. I count to ten as always, then carry him over to his car. And you know what?" He paused dramatically.

Straight said, "No, what?"

"There's a broad in the car." Coady laughed. "She seen the whole thing and her eyes is as wide as my mommy's cunt. She's so scared she could shit needles."

Coady started popping his knuckles one at a time. "So anyways," he continued, "I take her up to my room. She says she'll do anything only so long as I don't waste her. And she's not a bad-looking broad either. Man, I hit the jackpot that time. I mean to tell you I chapped her lips. I goddamned near choked her to death and saved myself the trouble of wasting her. But in the end I had to give her the old seven seconds. You know, that was one of the most frantic fucks I ever had. Get these broads scared enough and they sure know how to move."

Straight looked at him and wondered how McEachern expected him to teach Coady to be subtle.

Straight put on the plastic coat and Coady whistled.

"This is liable to be messy," Straight told him.

"Well, Spinoza, you do come equipped," said Coady. "That's the first time I ever see anything like that."

"Remember, same routine on the horn," Straight said.

"Sure," said Coady. "Beep, beep, beep. How long do you figure it to take?"

Straight shrugged. "Minutes."

Coady glanced at his watch and nodded. He would give Spinoza three minutes to get safely established in the house, then he'd go in after him.

Straight walked confidently to the front door of the Taber house. It was just after noon Thursday. Taber should be home for lunch almost immediately. The wife was on another unspecified mission to Oklahoma City.

Straight went through the door as quickly as if he had a key. He relocked it and went upstairs to the big bathroom. He removed the straight razor from its case, stepped into the shower stall and slid the door shut. He was betting Taber would hit the bathroom as soon as he got home.

Straight counted kills as he stood motionlessly in the shower stall. He was uneasy. This would be his thirteenth kill, an ominous number. He wasn't overly superstitious, but he had always figured his luck would run out on either the thirteenth job or the thirty-third. Thirteen for standard superstition; thirty-three for the age Christ died. Straight figured if he got through this one, he'd be safe for ten more years, at the rate of two jobs a year.

He stood in the shower wearing his plastic coat. The razor in his right hand dangled by his side.

Tracy Zantell smiled as the last customer left her small gift shop. She locked the door behind him and reversed the sign on the door which said "Open" on one side and "Closed" on the other. She quickly balanced the cash-register receipts. Then she donned a lightweight black-and-white coat and left the store. She made her daily deposit at the bank, smiling happily at the teller.

Back in her car she twisted the rear-view mirror around so she could see her face instead of the road behind her. She applied lipstick and checked her hair. Her short brown hair was immaculate. She paid $5.50 every Wednesday night to have it fixed, because Thursday afternoon was the most important time of her week. It was the afternoon Denise was out of town and she could have Arthur Taber to herself for hours.

Tracy put the mirror back in the proper position and started the engine. She tapped her fingers on the steering wheel in time to the music coming from the radio.

Lovely Thursday, Tracy thought.

Arthur Taber was fifty-nine years old, but on Thursday afternoons he felt forty. Nothing could destroy his good mood. He even managed to say "Same to you, friend" to the crank on the telephone without becoming upset.

Martha Henning, the salesgirl, looked over at her boss and smiled. "Another one?" she asked sympathetically.

Taber nodded. "Somebody I don't guess has ever been in the store is sure he knows how much it's worth. He actually called me a reactionary capitalist."

Martha giggled. "You hang in there, Mr. Taber. There hasn't been this much controversy in Solano for years."

Taber grinned lazily. "It is fun, isn't it?" he said. "This whole town's comprised of idiots. They run into one small difficulty and they're ready to give two hundred thousand dollars back to the feds. I don't see why they don't build their building on the edge of town. Christ, you'd think Solano was a metropolis the way they have to have the courthouse right downtown. They could build it five miles out of town, and it would still only take five minutes to get there from any point in Solano. Where's Rope?"

"He said he was going to play golf this afternoon," Martha said.

"Can you handle the store all right by yourself?"

"Sure, Mr. Taber. You go ahead."

Taber grinned at her and put on a gray hat. "Keep the faith," he said.

He drove home whistling.

Taber unlocked his front door and went upstairs. In the bedroom he shed his coat, hat and tie. Then he went into the large bathroom to wash up.

. . .

Coady waited three minutes after Taber had entered the house. Then he cracked his knuckles, flexed his hands, left the car and his lookout post and walked up to the front door.

The door was unlocked.

Careless man, Coady thought.

He stepped into the living room and shut the door quietly behind him. There was no sound in the house, but Spinoza had told him the hit would be upstairs. Coady located the staircase and had gone up three steps when he heard a door open in the rear of the house.

Quickly Coady ducked back down the stairs. He went through a door into a room with book-lined walls. He left the door open a crack and peered through it.

The woman in the black-and-white coat was in her mid-thirties, Coady guessed. She came out of the kitchen, slipped out of the coat and started unbuttoning her blouse as she hit the stairs. Coady's eyes widened as he saw a black brassiere, then the woman walked out of his line of vision.

Coady grinned. A problem for Spinoza. But then he sobered, for it was also a problem for him. The place was becoming too crowded. He didn't want to haul off more than one body.

Another time, another place, he thought. I can always waste him while he's reading one of them damn books.

Coady slipped out the front door and went back to the car.

Tracy stepped out of her skirt and slip and looked at her reflection in the mirror.

Not bad, she thought, not bad at all.

She had never made the mistake of having children, so her belly and thighs were still unscarred. And as long as she supported her breasts with a bra, they looked firm and youthful.

She stretched and rotated her hips. Watching the motion in the mirror increased her desire. She knocked on the bathroom door.

"Art? I've got something for you."

No response.

Tracy glanced at the clock. It was 12:20. Plenty of time for Art to get home.

She felt a sudden surge of fear. Maybe it was his heart. She rapped on the bathroom door again and tried the knob. It was locked.

Anxiously she went out into the hall to telephone.

Straight had just placed Taber's body headfirst in the shower stall when the knock on the door filled the bathroom.

Goddamn Coady to hell, Straight thought.

He froze and listened to a female voice call Art. Taber's blood made no noise as it trickled down the shower drain.

Straight leaned his head against the door and heard the indistinct sound of a telephone dial spinning back into place. He closed his eyes and visualized the house. There was no phone in the bedroom. But there was a telephone stand in the hall.

He left the razor in the shower by Taber's right hand and cautiously opened the door. The bedroom was empty.

Straight took off the plastic coat, reversed it and folded it so no blood would drip. He had taken four steps into the bedroom when he heard a rustling behind him. He turned his head impassively and traded stares with a huge black cat.

A black cat on the thirteenth job, Straight thought. Perfect.

He leaned against the bedroom wall and risked a glance into the hall. A woman in bra and panties was using the telephone. Her back was to him.

Straight immediately and silently took three steps across the hall and entered another bedroom. The woman was not speaking. In a moment he heard the sound of the dial rotating again.

Nobody home the first time, he thought. So she's not after the law.

"Is Mr. Taber there?" said the woman. "Oh. How long ago was that? All right, thank you."

Jewelry store, Straight thought. He willed the woman to return to the bedroom. Instead she went down the stairs. Her bare feet made no sound on the carpet.

Straight walked to the head of the stairs. The woman turned toward the back of the house. Garage, he thought. He went straight down the stairs and into the study. He heard a door close, and now he could hear the woman's footsteps.

She was running.

Found Taber's car, Straight thought.

As the woman went up the stairs, Straight went out the front door. He walked hurriedly to the rented car.

Coady started the engine and Straight slid in beside him. He set the plastic coat on the floorboard.

"Let's drift," Straight said calmly.

The bathroom door was open. Tracy didn't bother going in. She dressed and called the police.

Two

"I've got gastritis," Maneri said.

He stood in the doorway that connected his cubbyhole with Cranmer's office. Cranmer's suite in the Trinity Building on North May Avenue consisted of three rooms: a reception room, Cranmer's spacious office and Maneri's restricted area. The reception area contained four straight chairs with leather upholstery and the secretary's desk and chair. There was a painting on one wall which had been a gift from one of Maneri's vanquished OCU students. A distorted redhead who looked vaguely like Maneri dominated the picture, and there was an inky squid in the lower left corner that the girl said was supposed to represent Cranmer. As nearly as it is possible to make a squid appear friendly and appealing, the girl had made the squid appear friendly and appealing. Its tentacles surrounded Maneri.

Cranmer's office was fairly luxurious. A crushed-velvet couch, avocado-green, sat along one wall. A comfortable leather chair sat behind Cranmer's commodious desk, and there were two matching chairs placed in front of the desk for clients. A small bathroom adjoined Cranmer's office.

Maneri's cubicle held only a metal desk and a straight chair, plus a client chair which matched the couch in Cranmer's office. A portable stereo was on the floor opposite the green chair.

Two doors led from the hall to the suite—one to the reception area, one to Maneri's office. That way Maneri could come and go as he pleased. The door to Maneri's office was unmarked; the door to the reception area was labeled *Cranmer Investigations.*

Cranmer was sprawled on the avocado couch. He opened one eye when Maneri spoke and peered at the redhead groggily. "My God," he said, "is it really you?"

Maneri looked down at his gray suit and tie self-consciously. "I'm a businessman today," he explained.

Maneri was slender, but his compact body suggested strength. His hair was fashionably long, covering his ears and hanging to his shoulders.

Cranmer rubbed his eyes. "Gastritis, huh?" he mumbled. "You're moving in fast company, young Maneri. They put Bill Kilmer in the hospital a week or so ago with gastritis."

"The Redskin?"

"Correct. What did the sawbones have to say?"

Maneri held up a brown paper bag. "He said Vitamin D." He pulled a quart of milk out of the bag. "I'm actually supposed to drink this drivel." He set the milk on Cranmer's desk.

Cranmer hoisted himself off the couch and limped over to sit behind his desk. He sneered at the milk.

"It's been a rough day," Maneri sighed. "You ever have your stomach x-rayed?"

"Christ, no. I'm a picture of health."

"Sure you are. Well, it is strange. They stand you up on an x-ray table and make you suck away on a cup of barium. They rotate you into position, tell you to take six swallows of barium, then shoot a picture. They shift you around to every conceivable angle."

"I thought barium was a rock," Cranmer said.

"It tastes like it was drained off a rock. Pink-looking crap. Man, you wouldn't believe the diet I'm supposed to follow. I think my doctor's some kind of fanatic. All I can eat is boiled chicken."

Cranmer raised his right eyebrow.

"A simple hyperbole," Maneri said. "I'm not supposed to drink beer. Can you imagine that? The doctor said if I had to drink I should drink liquor. It's easier on the stomach."

Cranmer lit a Camel and blew smoke at Maneri. "I've an idea this diet will be short-lived," he said.

Maneri grinned. "Yeah. My gut doesn't hurt all that bad."

"What were the x-rays for?" Cranmer asked.

"They thought I had an ulcer. But—no holes. Just a nervous stomach."

Cranmer laughed at him. "I told you those goddamn women were getting to you."

Maneri lit a cigarette, sat down and braced his feet on Cranmer's desk. "Would you believe that freaky quack told me to quit smoking?" he said aggrievedly. "What does that have to do with my stomach?"

"Some doctors don't like smoke," Cranmer said. "I broke my foot once and a Washington medic told me it would heal better if I quit smoking. I never tested his theory."

Maneri reached inside his coat and tossed a mimeographed sheet of paper on Cranmer's desk, next to the quart of milk. "Scan that," he said.

Cranmer peered at the paper. "Oatmeal," he said. "Terrific. Looks like the old boil-and-broil route for you."

"Piss on it," said Maneri. "He gave me some pills to keep my stomach from churning out so much lethal shit. I'll let the pills do the work. Do you realize if I followed that diet I'd have to do my own cooking?"

"That would probably be more dangerous than booze and cigarettes," Cranmer agreed.

Maneri tossed the diet sheet in the trash. "Dallas was more subdued than usual," he said.

Cranmer nodded. "I read they only arrested a hundred and something. The year I went they pinched over four hundred."

"The rain dampened our spirits," said Maneri.

"The game dampened mine," said Cranmer. "What a joke! And to think I was afraid to bet on it."

"You watch it on TV?" Maneri asked.

"Natch. Tell you what. I bet OU really moves up in the national rankings now. If they'd played Southern Cal on TV, they'd already be up there."

"It do make a difference," Maneri said.

Cranmer stretched and yawned. "I hate to bring this up, Butch," he said, "but did you get to that warehouse yet?"

"Certainly." Maneri saluted. "Don't I look like a proper businessman?"

"You're lovely," said Cranmer. "Cook's due here at three. You can tell me what you found when you tell him."

"Yeah, I wouldn't want to wear you out," said Maneri. "I saw in the appointment book Sandusky came in. What's his pitch?"

Cranmer curled his lip. "He thought he was in a crooked card game. Don't know what the hell he expected me to do about it."

"You mean you didn't nick him for any cash?"

"Oh, I gave him a card lesson. Showed him how to deal seconds and told him what to watch for. I charged him fifty."

"Wow. You upped our tax bracket."

Cranmer was searching for a comeback when Cindy Dawson came into the office. The secretary was thirty-one years old and looked twenty-five: a trim figure, long black hair and arresting, translucent black eyes in which the pupils were barely discernible. She had been married three times and happily divorced each time. She was a luxury. Cranmer didn't really need a secretary, but he hated paperwork enough to pay Cindy for spending about six hours a day reading Gothic novels.

She treated both Cranmer and Maneri with such casual affection that, despite her attractiveness, neither of them had ever imagined making a pass at her.

"Hi, Butch," she said in a pleasantly low voice. "How's the tummy?"

"I've got gastritis," Maneri said.

"Figures," she said, winking at Cranmer. "There's a woman named Tracy Zantell here to see you," she announced.

Cranmer scowled. "She's not on my calendar," he complained.

"That doesn't mean she shouldn't be," Maneri said, dropping his feet to the floor.

"Quit picking on my secretary," Cranmer said proprietorially.

"She's quite good-looking," Cindy said in the nearly condescending tone of a woman secure in her own attractiveness.

Maneri applauded softly.

"What time is it?" said Cranmer.

"Ten till three," said Cindy.

"Tell her she'll have to wait. I'll talk to her after Cook leaves."

"I can take care of Cook," Maneri protested.

Cranmer shook his head. "It's more impressive if the star of the show is around," he said.

Maneri looked at the ceiling. Cindy went back to the outer office.

"By the way," said Cranmer, "don't mention anything to Cook about going to Dallas. He called Friday and I told him you were hard at work on his case."

"Well, I was working hard," said Maneri.

"Yeah, tearing holes in your stomach."

Cranmer grabbed his cane and limped into the bathroom. There was a bottle of pills on the back of the sink, a twin to the bottle in Cranmer's bathroom at home. Cranmer shook two of the round yellow tablets into his hand, bent over the sink and gurgled them down.

He limped back to his desk. "Pour some coffee," he said.

When Maneri delivered the coffee, Cranmer took a quart of bourbon out of a desk drawer and splashed some in his cup. He raised interrogative eyebrows at Maneri.

Maneri shook his head. "I'm not even supposed to drink coffee," he said, sipping.

Cindy opened the door and announced: "Mr. Cook."

A rotund middle-aged man in a conservative suit entered the office. Maneri left the chair in front of Cranmer's desk and sat on the couch. Cook sat down in the chair Maneri had vacated.

"Coffee?" offered Cranmer.

"No, thanks. Did you find anything?"

Cranmer nodded. "My man here has a report," he said. His eyes twinkled at Maneri.

Maneri lit a cigarette with a grand gesture. "Your suspicions were accurate, Mr. Cook," he said. "The Bismarck Company is a phony. I'd estimate they'll declare bankruptcy in a month.

"I went there as a prospective customer. And the shop just isn't set up right. Take watches, for example. They've got a pile of five-hundred-dollar watches and another pile of ten-dollar watches. But they've got nothing in between. Now, a legitimate business will stock all prices, right? But Bismarck is after stuff they can sell in bulk. Right now I'd say they were establishing their credit, with transactions like the hundred clock radios they bought from you. They paid promptly?"

Cook nodded. "And immediately placed another order—this time for three thousand."

"Yeah, they're trying to move too fast," Maneri said. "I sounded them out about transistor radios. If I buy four thousand radios, I can get them at less than half price. Of course, all I turned up was indications. I'm satisfied they're phony, but we'd never be able to prove it. It's tough to prove someone started a business with the intention of going bankrupt, even after they go broke. There's too many ways for them to dump the money."

"Well, I'm not after a conviction," Cook said. "I merely want to avoid being stuck for three thousand radios."

"Don't fill the order," said Maneri.

"We could put some pressure on them," Cranmer interjected. "I can call the head of the company and tell him we're wise. I'll tell him to pay off the three thousand radios or else I'll blow the whistle. That way you can make a profit."

Cook shook his head. "I wouldn't want to support crooks."

"Hell, you'll be taking money out of their pockets," said Cranmer. "They're not going to be able to unload those radios at the regular price. They'll have to take a loss."

"No, I don't think so," Cook said. "I'll simply refuse to fill the order, and I'll spread the word about the Bismarck Company. I thank you for confirming my doubts."

"We'll bill you," Cranmer said.

Cook shook hands and left the office.

"Guy's got no vision," Cranmer complained.

"He's honest," said Maneri. "I can understand how that would confuse you."

"Shit. It's not dishonest to rob robbers."

Cindy opened the door. "Will you see Tracy Zantell now?"

"Zip her in," said Cranmer.

Cranmer's Demerol had taken effect. His nose was tingling, and his body was suffused with a floating sensation. He had trouble focusing his eyes on the newspaper clipping Tracy Zantell had given him.

The clipping was from the *Medwick Herald.* The article had been written by Donald Dorne.

Cranmer finished the story and handed the clipping to Maneri. "Where is this Solano?" he asked.

Maneri carried the clipping over to the couch, slouched into a spineless position and said, "Near Medwick. Southwestern part of the state."

Cranmer nodded vaguely. He eyed Tracy Zantell approvingly and said, "Where do you fit into this, Miss Zantell?"

In reply she handed him another newspaper story. This one was brief and vague. It dealt with the suicide of Arthur Taber. The only meat in the article was the statement that police had determined the death to be suicide and the body had been discovered by Tracy Zantell, a neighbor. The remainder of the story was obituary information.

Cranmer flipped the clipping to Maneri.

"It wasn't suicide," said Tracy Zantell.

Cranmer lit a Camel. As always, the Demerol gave it a magic, wonderful flavor. He gazed fondly at Tracy Zantell. He liked her. The way he felt, he would have liked her if she had been a female wrestler.

"Why wasn't it suicide?" he asked lazily.

"Because it's simply ridiculous," Tracy said. "Art had never been happier. That controversy about his building stimulated him. Our dedicated marshal is trying to sell the story Art killed himself in a fit of remorse. That's bullshit."

Cranmer raised his eyebrows. Maneri grinned.

"You're saying because just because," Cranmer protested. "Do you have any valid reason for doubting the suicide theory?"

"I certainly do. Listen, that business in the paper about me being a neighbor is so much chaff. We were lovers. Every Thursday afternoon he'd stay home from work and I'd close my shop. His wife would be out of town and we'd spend the afternoon in bed at his house. The idea he'd pick that day to kill himself is nonsense. Even if he was depressed, he certainly wouldn't have chosen Thursday afternoon."

Cranmer tugged at his ear. "Tell me about finding him."

"It was last Thursday. I got to Art's house about twelve-fifteen. I undressed in the bedroom upstairs. There's a bathroom adjoining the bedroom. The door was closed, so I figured Art was in there. When I knocked on the bathroom door, there was no answer. The door was locked. Now, that's important—the door was locked. I was worried. Art had a mild heart condition —he was nearly sixty years old—and I was afraid he might have been stricken. But first I wanted to make sure he was home. I didn't think there was much doubt with the bathroom door locked, but after all, he was married, and if he was just late getting home, he certainly wouldn't have appreciated my stirring up a fuss. So I called his jewelry store. They said he was gone. Then I went downstairs and saw his car was in the garage. So I knew he was home, and I figured he was ill. When I got back upstairs, I went into the bedroom to dress before calling for help. And the bathroom door was ajar. I looked in and found him."

"You told this to the police?" Cranmer asked.

"Yes. Well, we don't really have police. We have a town marshal, a sheriff and a deputy. I told them."

"And they still called it suicide?"

"Sure. Because it was easier. It was the popular decision."

Cranmer looked at Maneri. Maneri shrugged.

"How did they explain the door being open?" asked Cranmer.

Tracy's face turned red. "Are you ready for this? They said a cat opened it."

"A cat!"

"That's right. Art had a big black cat named Orestes. And the thing about it is Orestes *can* open the bathroom door from the inside. The door has one of those knobs you push in and turn to lock. Orestes could jump against the door and shake it loose. Art and Denise used to show him off when they had company. They'd lock him in the bathroom upstairs, go back down to the party, and in no time at all Orestes would be downstairs begging scraps. Jamie Darden, the marshal, had been there before and seen Orestes in action. So he didn't even hesitate about how the door got unlocked."

Cranmer splashed some bourbon in his coffee cup. "Drink?" he asked.

"Please."

Maneri put some coffee in a cup, and Cranmer filled it with bourbon and handed it to Tracy.

"What's your theory, Miss Zantell?" Cranmer asked.

"One of those simple-minded bastards killed him," she said bluntly. "I think whoever it was, was still in the bathroom with him when I knocked on the door. Then he sneaked out and left the door open behind him."

"You can lock the door from both sides?"

"That's right. It takes a key to open it from the outside."

"Well, then, why wouldn't your killer just lock the door back?"

"Panic," she said firmly. "When I knocked on the door, he must have been terrified."

Cranmer made an indecipherable sound. "You figure someone killed him because he wouldn't sell his jewelry store?" he asked.

"I'm sure of it. You wouldn't believe how angry the people in Solano were with Art. They said terrible things."

Maneri said, "They may have said terrible things, but it takes a strong stomach to cut somebody's throat. Even if they hit him at arm's length with that straight razor, blood would have spurted all over the place."

Tracy paled.

"Sorry," said Maneri. "Just making a point."

"What makes you the avenging angel, Miss Zantell?" Cranmer asked. "Taber had a couple of decades on you. Are you trying to say it was all for love and not the bankroll?"

She laughed. Cranmer, who had been trying to make her mad, scowled at her.

"Love isn't a thing I believe in," Tracy said. "But I place a high value on loyalty. Everybody in town is glad Art's dead. I want to make them squirm."

Cranmer shrugged. "I guess we can go over there and stir things around, but I doubt we'll accomplish much. I want you to go into this with your eyes open."

"They're open."

"Who sent you here?" Cranmer asked.

"Nobody sent me. There aren't any detectives in Solano. I picked you out of the phone book."

"I'm not in the phone book," Cranmer said.

"Like hell." Tracy picked up a phone book from Cranmer's desk and started leafing through it.

"Yeah, okay, I'm in the book," said Cranmer.

Maneri grinned brightly at him from the couch.

"I'm glad you don't seem eager," said Tracy. "If you jumped at it, I'd figure you were trying to fleece me."

"It'll cost you," Cranmer muttered.

"I'll pay. Nobody dies that conveniently."

Cranmer scratched his nose. "We might meet a little opposition if we go out there as employees of Taber's mistress," he said. "Did Taber have any life insurance?"

She said yes and named a company.

"Okay," Cranmer said. "We'll be insurance investigators. Anyway, I will. You know anybody in Solano, Butch?"

Maneri nodded. "Yeah, I know one of the county commissioners. Want me to get a job?"

"Can you?"

"Sure. This guy owes me a little something."

"All right, we'll do it that way," Cranmer decided. He explained to Tracy, "If Butch goes undercover, he'll find out a lot more in the field of gossip than I could. It'll cost you more, but it should be worth it."

"You handle it," said Tracy.

"It would help if I had some kind of a cover to go under," Maneri said. "You got anything in the way of relatives, Tracy?"

She shrugged. "Say you're my nephew. I've got a sister in California."

"Where in California?"

"La Puente. That's a suburb . . ."

"Yeah, I've been there," said Maneri. "Let me have your address and phone number in Solano."

She provided the information.

"I'll come see you when I get settled," Maneri said.

"When can you start, Mr. Cranmer?" she asked.

"Oh, I'll be there in a couple of days. I've got a few things to wrap up here first."

Tracy stood up. "Anything else?"

Cranmer shook his head. "You can fill me in on the people when I get there."

She shook hands with Cranmer and Maneri and left the office.

"A lady with a mission," Cranmer sighed.

"Well, you made a good try at getting out of the job," Maneri said.

"Yeah. She likes people who aren't eager. Batshit. A cat that opens doors. Remind me to take plenty of whiskey."

August McEachern was sixty-four years old. He had attained that ripe old age in his hazardous profession because he was a highly suspicious and highly cautious man. But for years Richard Straight had been an albatross wearing down his nervous system.

"I don't trust that Straight any further than I can throw my left eye," McEachern would say to his man Friday, Harold.

"Yes, sir, Mr. McEachern," Harold would say.

Finally McEachern decided Straight's skills weren't worth the price of Tums, and he put out the ironic contract on him.

Now McEachern was seething. "Coady bollixed it," he told Harold. "He says he followed Straight into the house to do the job, and a woman came through the back door. Coady panicked and darted back outside. Straight sauntered out a few moments later. But even Straight's kill wasn't clean. Coady says when he went back outside, there was a car parked up the street with a man in it. A car that hadn't been there before."

"Yes, sir, Mr. McEachern," said Harold. "What now?"

"When Straight called me, I told him to stay put with Coady until he was sure the kill wouldn't have any repercussions. Rimson told Coady to wait until everything died down and then wipe out Straight. Jesus, Harold, there just aren't any professionals any more."

"Yes, sir, Mr. McEachern," said Harold.

Tracy Zantell reached over to the bedside table, snared a cigarette and lit it. "That was very nice," she said.

"It was more than nice," said Michael Rope. He scratched the graying hair on his chest. "Let's get married," he said. "We could have this all the time."

"Why get married? You don't have to marry for this."

Rope propped himself up on an elbow. He was fortyish. His crew cut was mostly gray. "Don't you ever get lonely?"

"Never. I like to be alone, and I'm not lonely when I am."

Rope sighed. "You'll give in one of these days," he prophesied.

Tracy stubbed out half a cigarette. "Where were you Thursday noon?" she asked. "I tried to call you when I got worried about Art."

Rope collapsed onto his back again. "Playing golf."

"Big businessman, huh?"

Rope murmured and fell asleep.

Tracy closed her eyes and saw Art Taber's throat. She got out of bed and went to the bathroom to clean up.

Cranmer punched the buttons on his desk telephone.

"Wally? Cough it up, friend."

"Hello, Steve. What are you crowing about? You only won a hundred."

"That's so, but I feel confident. I think I'll match that tonight."

"Which way do you want to go?" asked Wally.

"What's the line?"

"Miami's giving nine."

"Nine points? Hell, I may bet my life savings. They're playing in Cleveland, aren't they?"

"Right."

"Sold. Put a hundred on Cleveland for me. Did Maneri hit on any of his wild parlays?"

"Nah. But he wasn't too wild this time. He bet the same teams on a parlay you bet on straight bets. Southern Cal, Missouri and Michigan State, right?"

"South Carolina instead of Southern Cal," Cranmer said.

"Yeah, I always get them mixed up. You hear what Michigan State did to you?"

"They fumbled nine times. No wonder they got slaughtered. I hope they lose all the rest of their games."

Wally laughed. "Don't say that. You may want to bet on them again. You going to bet on the Series?"

"Haven't made up my mind yet. I have to go out of town this week, so I may pass it up. You figure Oakland?"

"I'd never bet against those crazy Mets," said Wally.

"Yeah. You bring the hundred by tonight."

"All right. I may get over there to watch the game with you."

"I'll be home," Cranmer said.

Cranmer cradled the receiver and pushed a buzzer. In a minute Cindy Dawson walked into the office.

"You rang?" she said archly.

"You want some time off?" Cranmer asked.

"With pay?"

Cranmer laughed. "You know there's always a catch. No, Butch and I are going down to Solano for a few days. Not much point in keeping the office open."

"I'd rather work," she said.

"Oh, hell, I'll still pay you," Cranmer said. "Go ahead and send Cook a bill and you can go home."

"How much?"

Cranmer scratched his nose. "Charge him two days agency and one Maneri," he decided. "Say Maneri worked half a day Friday and half a day Monday."

The secretary left. Cranmer picked up his cane and limped after her. Solano could wait till after the ball game.

Maneri glared at the glass of milk, then used it to wash down a pill. He grimaced. He placed a hand on his stomach and tried to convince himself the beer he had just finished had not made him uncomfortable.

Earlier in the afternoon he had called McIntosh Johnson, one of the county commissioners of Solano County, and been promised a job on the road crew. The work seemed unpalatable to Maneri, but it would be a switch. Fresh air and sunshine might not necessarily prove fatal. And in a town like Solano, a laboring position drew unquestioned trust and respect.

Maneri shoved the quart of milk into the refrigerator. His apartment was a one-bedroom affair with a thick gold shag carpet. The walls were covered with velvety paper. The furniture was modern and well coordinated. Maneri invested over a bill and a half per month in rent, and he was content.

It had not always been that way. Before Maneri hooked up with Cranmer, he had lived from day to day. His major source of income in those days had been shooting pool. He still shot a wicked game, but now Cranmer found assignments which were suited to his particular talents.

Maneri was not a partner in the detective agency, although he had an office in Cranmer's suite. He did not yearn for the responsibility of showing up at an office every day. He stayed on call. And Cranmer understood that if Maneri wanted to go to Miami for a weekend rather than investigate, Maneri would go to Miami. But once Maneri accepted a case, he saw it through to completion.

Maneri pulled the pop top of another can of Schlitz and curled up on the couch in his living room. The voice of Hudie Ledbetter filled the room with "Dekalb Blues." Maneri sipped his beer and decided that as long as he refused to worry about his stomach, it wouldn't bother him.

There was a knock at the door. Maneri made a face and went to answer.

Gail Hand, Maneri's companion on his trip to Dallas, was an attractive brunette in her early twenties. Although she was not tall, she had long, pliant legs—her greatest asset. Gail lived downstairs. She was divorced, had a little daughter and worked as a secretary at Tinker Air Force Base.

Maneri said, "Come on in," and returned to his couch.

Gail sat in the matching chair and stretched her legs out before her. Despite the cool weather, she wore a tight pair of white shorts. Her Mickey Mouse T-shirt made it evident she wore no bra.

"Have you recovered from Dallas yet?" she asked. Her voice was a nasal twang.

"I've got gastritis," Maneri said.

"You're kidding," she protested. "You're too young to have gastritis. I had an uncle who got it when he was about sixty."

"I feel sixty most of the time," Maneri said.

"Are you on a diet? No fried foods and all that?"

"Well, supposedly." Maneri sucked on his beer.

Gail stretched and yawned, arching her back sensually. Maneri watched the movement of her breasts with frank admiration. "God, I didn't think four o'clock was ever going to get here," she said. "I feel like I've been up for a week. And we didn't turn a tap all day. Did you work?"

"Yeah, some," Maneri said. "I've got to go to Solano tomorrow, spend a few days."

"What's in Solano?"

"A murder. Or maybe a suicide. That's what we're supposed to find out."

"What kind of murder?"

"A mysterious one. That's what I do, you know, solve mysteries."

"I suppose that means you can't take us to dinner tomorrow night," Gail pouted.

" 'Fraid so. Want to do it tonight?"

"Ruthie's over at her grandmother's."

Maneri grinned. "Perfect," he said.

She frowned. "That's not nice."

"This is." Maneri slid open a drawer in the coffee table and pulled out a crumpled hand-rolled cigarette. The joint resembled a snake that had swallowed a chicken. Maneri lit the swollen end, took a deep drag, held it, then exhaled explosively. "Here," he said, extending the joint to Gail, "this should knock out your hangover."

Gail accepted the joint and puffed lightly.

They passed the joint back and forth and spoke languorously about their weekend in Dallas. Maneri replaced the Leadbelly record with José Feliciano, and they listened to a flamboyant version of "Hey Jude."

"It's fantastic," Maneri said dreamily. "When he hits a chord, I can hear him strike each individual string."

Gail nodded, stood up and walked precariously over to Maneri's couch. She sat beside him, cuddled up to him. Maneri's tongue felt swollen. He kissed Gail leisurely, interminably, and felt the first vague stirrings of desire in his groin.

"Let's go to bed," he murmured. "I have to rise early in the morning, don my Batman suit and venture into the world to fight crime."

Gail giggled. "It's barely five," she said.

Maneri stood up and peeled off his shirt. His body was flat, muscular and pale. "I need a lot of sleep," he said. "I'm a growing boy."

Ham Coady stared at Straight in astonishment.

"What the fuck're you doing?" he demanded.

Straight had installed a hot plate in their room in Medwick's Gentry Hotel. He had just finished boiling a cup of water and was starting to sip it. The FM radio was playing a Beethoven string quartet.

Straight returned Coady's stare impassively. "I've discovered a new coffee that's one hundred percent caffeine-free," he said.

Coady shook his head. "I think you've gone bananas," he decided. "Reminds me of this one job I pulled in Birmingham. The target there was this cat what drunk straight grain alcohol. I think it was getting to him and that's why the contract went out. That was one of the times I knocked some cat off from a distance. This clown had a fucking bodyguard. So I blew him apart with a Mauser."

"Peter Paul Mauser," Straight said, sipping his boiled water.

"Nah, it was a regular repeater, Spinoza," said Coady. "I was in and out of Birmingham in one day. They already had me an apartment rented across the street from this cat's pad. I come into town, set up, blammo, and beat it. Somehow it didn't seem like I really wasted the guy. I don't like that long-distance stuff."

"Talk for less than a minute after midnight and save," Straight said.

"Sure."

Straight went back to Kierkegaard.

"How long you figure we gotta hang around this dump?" asked Coady.

Straight shrugged. "They'll be in touch."

Miami scored a late touchdown to increase their lead to 17–9. Cranmer swallowed two more Demerols. He hated squeakers. But Miami had no intention of trying to run up the score. They were satisfied to run out the clock, and they made Cranmer a gift of a hundred dollars.

Cranmer downed his bourbon and water and started riding Wally. "I'm going to break your book," he said.

Wally laughed. "Hate to disappoint you, Steve, but there was a lot more bet on Miami than Cleveland. It came out fine."

Cranmer walked out to the kitchen of his spacious three-bedroom house and fixed drinks. Logically, the house was much too large for Cranmer. But he liked space and was willing to pay for it.

The television was in the den. One wall of the den consisted of a fireplace. An artificial log burned in it. Cranmer preferred real fires, but he could think of no way to have one without going to the trouble of building it.

"How's the leg?" Wally asked.

"Stiff. These chilly nights tighten it up."

"Chilly! Man, you're in for a world of trouble when it actually gets cold."

Cranmer swallowed bourbon. "I'll just stay inside," he said.

When Wally left, Cranmer went into the bedroom, donned pajamas and crawled into bed to read. He read one chapter of *Pig Sale*, a book dealing with an interesting innovation in the white-slave trade, then remembered to call Maneri.

Maneri's voice was filled with sleep. "You call Solano?" Cranmer asked.

"Yeah, dad. I start work tomorrow. On a road crew."

Cranmer laughed. He heard a feminine voice in the background. "Saying good-bye?" he asked Maneri.

"I'd like to say good-bye to you," Maneri muttered.

"Leave messages with your aunt," Cranmer ordered.

The feminine voice said something unintelligible and Maneri hung up.

Cranmer returned to *Pig Sale*. But the bourbon and Demerol had taken their effect, and he couldn't focus on the page. He doused the light and watched the black ceiling move.

Maneri's alarm clock crashed at 4:30 A.M. He opened his eyes and gazed disgustedly at the darkness for a minute, then forced himself out of bed and went across to the dresser to switch off the alarm. He had the clock positioned in such a way that he was required to leave his bed to silence it. He had learned that if it was by his bedside, he could stab it off and go back to sleep all in one motion.

Maneri poured himself a glass of milk and took some medicine. He tossed an assortment of clothes into a brown airline bag and was on the road to Solano by five.

Maneri loved driving at night. He could let his Fiat go with relatively little fear of the consequences. The speed coupled with the narrow world of the headlights created a heady sensation. He shoved a home-grown Dylan tape into the tape player. The Fiat was wired for sound. One of Maneri's pool-shooting friends worked at Stereo City, and he had provided Maneri with an excellent selection of speakers. There were four of them in the car: one in each door, one on each side of the shelf behind the rear seat. Dylan's voice came from the left rear and his harmonica wailed from the passenger door.

Maneri covered the 160 miles to Solano in just over two hours. By 7:30 he had located McIntosh Johnson's house in the country.

Johnson was drinking coffee. He rose at five every morning, puttered around the farm for a couple of hours, then chain-drank coffee until it was time to hit the courthouse. He had been a Solano county commissioner for eighteen years.

He gave Maneri a cup of coffee. "It's been a while, Butch," he said. "You say you're in the City now?"

"Too true," said Maneri. "I turned respectable."

Johnson laughed. "I'm glad to see you shaved the beard. I got to thinking after you called yesterday, it wouldn't make too good of an impression down here."

"I haven't worn it for a while," Maneri said. "Seemed like I was always ending up with hair in my mouth."

"Believe it or not, I had a beard once," Johnson said. "Of course, that was back in the depression, and nobody thought anything about it. It wasn't unusual to not be able to buy razor blades back then. Mine was always pretty scraggly."

"Same as your head, huh?" said Maneri.

Johnson rubbed his bald spot and grinned. "What are you up to, Butch?" he asked. "You're not planning to make a career of repairing roads, are you?"

"It's good honest work," Maneri said, deadpan.

"That's why I don't figure you'd be interested."

"Ouch. No, Mac, truth to tell, I'm a claims investigator for an insurance company now. Keep that under your hard hat, though. I'm down here to see about a character named Taber."

Johnson nodded. "Yeah, Art Taber. I knew him a long time. Never figured him to kill himself. I mean, he was so tight it'd take a tractor to pull a needle out of his ass. People like that usually last forever. But what's to investigate?"

"Routine," Maneri improvised. "We're always skeptical of suicides—especially when it brings in forty thousand dollars."

Johnson whistled. "I didn't think insurance would pay off on a suicide."

"Depends on the time," Maneri said. "Taber's policy had a three-year suicide clause, but he'd had it over ten years."

Johnson poured more coffee.

"By the way," said Maneri, "do you know a Tracy Zantell?"

"Sure. Runs a little gift shop. She come to town about the same time the Tabers did, if I remember right."

"She's my aunt," Maneri said.

Johnson raised an eyebrow. "If you say so. Funny you never went to see her when you were chasing after my daughter, though."

"How is Heather?" Maneri asked.

"Fat and happy. Two kids."

Maneri shook his head. "What a waste."

"There was some rumors floating around about your 'aunt' and Taber," Johnson said. " 'Course, they's always rumors in this town, but still and all, they sometimes turn out right."

Maneri grinned. "They're probably true," he said. "Sensuality runs in the family."

Johnson stood up. "Time to move," he said.

"One other thing," said Maneri. "You got an empty barn or something where I can stow my car? It's a little too hot for a road worker."

"No problem," said Johnson. "But how'll you get around?"

"Oh, I'll find some wheels."

Maneri put the Fiat in Johnson's garage. Then he clambered into the county commissioner's pickup and headed for his new job.

. . .

Cranmer's hand was shaking. He watched it with bright interest.

Well, it's better than gastritis, he thought.

He went into the bathroom and swallowed two Demerols. After the pills had soothed his system, he shaved and dressed.

Cranmer called the bus station. A 1:30 bus would get him to Norman by 2:10. He would have plenty of time to talk to the architect before the 3:45 bus left Norman for Solano.

Cranmer packed his clothes, then shrugged into his shoulder holster and checked the action of his .32 Colt. He put a two-shot derringer and a sleeve holster in his suitcase.

A cab ferried him to the bus station. In the lobby of the bus station he took two more pills to brace him for the bus ride. Cranmer hated buses.

The trip to Norman didn't alter his philosophy. The man in the seat next to him was an amateur politician who kept a running monologue going all the way to Norman on the evils of the ex-vice-president. Agnew had given a speech on television the previous night in which he had reaffirmed his innocence. Cranmer's seatmate couldn't picture a man pleading guilty in court and innocent on TV. Cranmer couldn't have cared less.

He shook the politician in Norman and rode to Jeremiah Kilduff's office in a taxi.

Kilduff's office was on Gray Street, one block off Main. It was a small building next to an air-conditioner outlet. The building was white frame and looked older than the paving on the street. Cranmer walked into the office. The floor was bare, and the walls and ceiling were cracked. It looked like a small-time divorce lawyer's office.

A man pushed his chair away from a drawing table and came to greet Cranmer. He was slender, about thirty, and wore a green eyeshade. Cranmer thought he looked like a blackjack dealer.

They shook hands and introduced themselves. Cranmer told Kilduff he was with the company that had insured Arthur Taber.

"Sit down," said Kilduff.

Cranmer sat in a rickety chair. "Taber had a fairly large life insurance policy," he said. "There seem to be a few details that don't fit right, so the company sent me out to take a look. I'd like to learn something about this building controversy he was involved in."

"He was a chicken-shit," Kilduff said emphatically. "We built a whole program around the assumption—no, not an assumption, a promise—he would sell his store to us. I don't know if you're familiar with the procedure of attaining a federal grant, Mr. Cranmer, but it's quite complicated. We worked on it for months. The grant finally came through and I designed a building for them. Then Taber decided he wanted more money. See, he waited until he thought we'd have too much invested, both in time and money, to argue with him. But those folks in Solano can be just as stubborn as Taber. They told him to go piss up a rope. I've been trying like hell to get them to consider another location, but they won't. They're mad now, and they'd rather see the whole project sink."

"Has Taber's death changed anything?" Cranmer asked.

Kilduff shrugged. "Too early to tell. I imagine it depends on whether or not the estate has to be probated. I've heard some casual gossip which indicates Mrs. Taber would be glad to unload the store. But I can't say that for a fact."

Cranmer tapped the floor with his cane. "If they cancel the project, it'd take some money out of your pocket, wouldn't it?"

"Yes. I'd still charge them for my time so far, but I'd lose the building."

"How much do you get from a deal like that?" Cranmer asked.

"Six percent," Kilduff said shortly.

Cranmer looked around the room and figured $12,000 would at least buy a carpet and some wallpaper.

"Any chance Taber might have been murdered because he wouldn't sell?" Cranmer asked.

"Murdered!" Kilduff looked shocked. "I thought it was a clear case of suicide."

"Suicides can be faked," Cranmer said carelessly. "Seems a lot of people were upset with Taber."

"My God," said Kilduff. "There's quite a difference between being upset with someone and murdering him."

Cranmer shrugged. "Not as much as you might think, sometimes," he said. "But you don't think it's likely, huh?"

"Definitely no."

Cranmer pulled a small notebook from his inside jacket pocket. "Let's see," he mused. "Taber died Thursday around noon. Would you mind telling me where you were at that time, Mr. Kilduff?"

Kilduff became nervous and angry simultaneously. "It so happens I have an alibi, Mr. Cranmer, if that's what you're hinting for."

"I didn't realize I was hinting," Cranmer said. "What's your alibi?"

"I was at a luncheon. A Kiwanis luncheon."

"Here in Norman?"

"That's right."

Cranmer wrote it down because he figured an insurance investigator would keep notes. Then he heaved himself to his feet and thanked Kilduff for his time.

"Oh, one more thing," he said. "You know anything about a woman in Solano named Tracy Zantell?"

Kilduff shook his head. "I worked mostly with the mayor and the city manager," he said. "Peter Brindle and John Fairchild. They're really the only people I know in Solano. Hell, I didn't really know Taber. I saw him at a council meeting once, is all."

"All right," Cranmer said. "Thanks."

Cranmer got back to the bus station in plenty of time to make a couple of telephone calls. He stretched his right leg out of the booth, inserted a dime and dialed.

Harry Colby answered his own phone. He was an automobile dealer who occasionally played poker with Cranmer. He told Cranmer what he knew about Kilduff, which wouldn't fill many volumes, and confirmed the architect had been at the Kiwanis luncheon the previous Thursday.

"How's his business?" Cranmer asked.

"Can't say. I can't think of any work he's done locally, but that doesn't mean he's not busy."

They exchanged banalities for a while, then Cranmer placed a collect call to Cindy Dawson. He asked her to earn at least a portion of her paycheck by running a financial check on Kilduff.

She agreed on the condition that Cranmer would pay her back for the phone call.

Cranmer took two more Demerols for the bus ride to Solano.

The land between Oklahoma City and Norman was flat, colorless, lifeless. And since that barren stretch of landscape was all many visitors to Oklahoma saw, it was little wonder they were in no rush to return. Dignitaries who landed at Will Rogers in Oklahoma City and rode in limousines to the University of Oklahoma in Norman could castigate the Sooner State with some authority, but the twenty-mile stretch was hardly typical.

Not that the rest of Oklahoma would be an inspiration to landscape painters, Cranmer thought, as his bus headed southwest toward Solano. But at least the terrain changed from flat to rolling and an occasional clump of stunted blackjacks or cottonwoods interrupted the monotony. One could see cattle, primarily Herefords and Angus, grazing stolidly in the pastures, and there were a few horses and, rarely, goats and pigs. Cranmer knew nothing of livestock. The only way he cared about a cow was to eat it.

At the second stop from Norman a middle-aged woman with erratically dyed hair and shredded stockings entered the bus and sat beside Cranmer. For the remainder of the journey she regaled him with tedious stories about her ex-husband, or husbands, Cranmer didn't listen closely enough to be sure.

He escaped the woman at Solano.

Solano was a typical Oklahoma small town. There was no bus station per se: the bus regurgitated Cranmer in front of a greasy restaurant called the T-P. Cranmer retrieved his suitcase and surveyed his new environment.

The business section, if such a grandiose name would apply to the dusty row of shabby stores, ran for five blocks. Cranmer spotted the jewelry store, tavern and barbershop he had read about in the *Medwick Herald.* Two blocks away from the T-P, Cranmer saw a battered sign: *Solano Inn.*

With his suitcase in his right hand and his cane in his left, Cranmer limped to the motel. He reserved a room for the princely sum of four dollars a day, left the office and peered at the motel with disapprobation. The motel's rooms made up three sides of a square. The fourth side consisted of the small office and a shabby club, which was closed. There was no swimming pool. The paint that hadn't peeled off the wooden motel units was so faded as to be colorless.

Four cars were parked in front of units. Cranmer read their bumper stickers and shook his head slowly. Three of the bumpers bore Nixon stickers. The other wore a Wallace tag. Next to "Honk If You Love Jesus" was a decal reading "Impeach Earl Warren."

The television in Cranmer's unit, number six, was black and white. He scowled at it. Baseball on TV was bad enough; he couldn't imagine it without color. He called Tracy Zantell.

"The troops are here," he said. "I'm at the Solano Inn, and Maneri's working for the county. Heard from him yet?"

"Not a murmur."

"Well, he'll be in touch. When can we get together?"

"I've got a date tonight. How about lunch tomorrow?"

Cranmer sighed. He had been hoping to wangle an invitation for a meal and a ball game. "Lunch at your place?" he said.

She laughed. "You don't want to be seen in public with Art Taber's mistress?"

"Nothing personal. I do think it would get in the way if people found out who I was working for."

"Make it about twelve-fifteen," she said.

"Done. If you see Maneri, or hear from him, tell him I'm in room six at the palace here."

Cranmer left the motel and ate a greasy steak for supper. Then he returned to watch Tom Seaver and Catfish Hunter go after each other—in black and white.

The Mets had Hunter on the ropes in the first inning, but they let him off and it eventually cost them the ball game, 3–2 in eleven innings.

Cranmer finished his bourbon and wished he had bet on Oakland. He was restless, even after ingesting the combination of bourbon and Demerol. Disenchantment with his surroundings was the only reason he could conjure. He grabbed his cane and his quart of Weller's and headed for the club in the motel.

It looked like a place the health inspectors visited annually.

Cranmer thought he could see rat urine fluorescing along the walls. He paid a dowdy barmaid seventy-five cents to put some water, frozen and liquid, in his bourbon.

There were fifteen or twenty people in the place. Most were watching the action at the one pool table. Cranmer sat at the bar with three men and one woman. Nobody was making conversation.

This would make a swell spot for a Schlitz commercial, Cranmer thought. He had to listen to "Easy Lovin' " three times before he could dispose of his drink. Then he heard a familiar voice behind him.

Cranmer rotated his barstool so he could face the pool table. Maneri was shooting. Cranmer watched him run the balls off the table, then sit at a table surrounded by a group of seven young men. Cranmer shook his head. Maneri worked fast. In a week he'd know the whole town.

The barmaid carried a can of beer over to Maneri. She had said only two words to Cranmer when she served him, but she laughed and joked with Maneri.

When Maneri headed for the bathroom, Cranmer walked in after him.

"Hi, dad," said Maneri.

Cranmer leaned against the door to keep it shut. "Have you solved it yet?" he asked sourly.

Maneri grinned at him. "No, but I heard a really lousy joke."

"Terrific," said Cranmer.

"Guy that runs a massage parlor is talking to the broads who do the rubbing," Maneri said. "He tells them they're supposed to give every single part of the customers a good massage. So this one young girl asks him, 'How about the genitals?' And he says, 'Treat them just like the Jews.' "

Maneri zipped his pants. He laughed at the expression on Cranmer's face. "I'll let you know when I hear a better one," he promised.

"Don't bother," said Cranmer. "You find a place to stay?"

"I'm going to spend tonight with Jerry Blefary, one of my hard-working road-gang companions. Tomorrow, who knows?"

"Well, I'm in room six if you need me," Cranmer said.

Maneri nodded. "Later," he said. He left.

Cranmer read the bathroom walls for a while to give Maneri time to get back to his table. The only memorable statement he saw was: "Fighting for freedom in Vietnam is like fucking for virginity." Cranmer didn't see the relationship but he liked the rhythm.

He picked up W. L. Weller and returned to his room.

Three

Peter Brindle, Solano's mayor, had his head stuck inside a television set. All Cranmer could see were cowboy boots, blue overalls and a blue denim shirt.

Cranmer lit a Camel and waited till Brindle emerged. He introduced himself. Brindle shifted a screwdriver from his right hand to his left and shook hands. He was a husky, balding man with a deep tan. Cranmer saw a large tackle box in the corner of the room and guessed Brindle spent a lot of time on the banks of ponds and streams. White eyebrows contrasted vividly with the mayor's tan. His voice was low and vibrant and he spoke in a lazy drawl.

"Be with you in just a minute," Brindle said and disappeared into the television again.

Cranmer leaned on his cane and blew smoke around the small workshop. He tried to accept the fact that Brindle was a mayor. He seemed more like the man who cleans up the street after a circus parade.

Brindle turned on the TV, spun the channel knob and gazed at the picture with satisfaction. "That oughta get it done," he said. He screwed the back plate of the TV into place, then turned to Cranmer. "Now," he said, "what can I do for you?"

Cranmer handed him a card. Brindle scanned it and said, "Insurance, huh? I've got more than I need."

"I'm not a salesman," said Cranmer. "I'm investigating the death of Arthur Taber."

Brindle's lips contracted in a false smile. "Let's go drink a cup," he suggested.

They left the TV repair shop and walked across Solano's main street to the T-P café. Cranmer noticed the main street was cleverly named "Main Street."

Cranmer sipped coffee and ran through his spiel about suspicious suicides.

Brindle seemed unconcerned. "Well, Mr. Cranmer," he said, "I see where you might have a problem, but what does it have to do with me? I knew Art, of course, but we certainly weren't close enough that I'd know if he was planning to call it quits."

"I'm interested in this building project," Cranmer said.

Brindle frowned. "I don't see where that fits."

Cranmer told him. Brindle recited the history of the controversy over Taber's building without telling Cranmer anything he didn't already know.

"Is the widow going to sell?" asked Cranmer.

Brindle shrugged. "Hopefully. We're holding off on returning the grant till she decides."

"Have you talked to her about it?"

"Not yet. Didn't seem like a good time for a business committee to go calling. We'll give it about a week."

Cranmer nodded and signaled the waitress for a refill. He said, "What's the widow, Denise, like?"

"A fine woman," Brindle said.

Cranmer scowled. "I know that's what you'd say as the mayor," he complained. "What would you say as a man?"

"I don't separate the two," Brindle said stiffly.

Cranmer needled the mayor a little more but couldn't get anything specific out of him. By the time they parted, Cranmer had accepted Brindle as a politician.

Cranmer walked down the main street a block to the city manager's office. Solano's city hall was a relic that predated WPA: a one-story red frame building. Cranmer realized why Solano wanted new quarters for the public officials.

John Fairchild, a swarthy, red-faced man, was cooperative but not helpful. He showed Cranmer copies of the grant application and a blueprint of the proposed building. He had only good words to say about the citizens of Solano.

Cranmer left the City Hall with no more satisfaction than if he had paid a water bill.

The Solano Inn was located at the west end of Main Street. Cranmer limped back to his room, turned on the TV and waited for noon. He was beginning to be skeptical of Tracy Zantell's theory that someone had killed Arthur Taber because he refused to sell his jewelry store.

"You're the only one who seems upset," Cranmer told Tracy Zantell. "The people I've talked to so far look at this jewelry store hassle as a simple business transaction. The only one who admitted irritation with Taber was the architect—and he stood to lose some money."

"You don't expect them to tell you about it, do you?" Tracy said indignantly.

Cranmer sighed. "The thing of it is," he said, "people don't go around knocking each other off without a valid reason. This building deal just doesn't seem like a valid motive to me. People kill for passion or gain. Not for abstracts like a new courthouse or city hall. It's not going to ruin the mayor's life or the city manager's life if that building isn't built."

Tracy shook her head. "They weren't the ones who were bitter. Talk to Sam Archer and Anthony Tomas—the men who own the businesses adjoining Art's. You say people kill for gain. Well, they both stood to gain if the deal went through. And they were both plenty mad at Art."

"I'll talk to them," Cranmer said. "But I still think you're off the track. Next thing I'm going to do is talk with this deputy or marshal or whatever about his cat theory. If I don't find something that indicates murder, I may go back home and save you some money."

"It seems to me you give up easily," Tracy said coldly.

"I don't like my motel room," Cranmer said carelessly. "You got any bourbon?"

Tracy fixed him a drink. They left the remains of lunch and went into the living room.

Tracy flashed some thigh at Cranmer as she sat down.

Cranmer said, "Tell me about the widow."

"A bitch," Tracy said bluntly. "She's been sleeping around on

Art for years. Every Monday and Thursday she goes up to Oklahoma City and shacks up."

"Who with?" asked Cranmer.

"Nobody knows. Art didn't care, and he never tried to find out. Said he was too old to worry about it."

"And anyway, you were taking care of him," Cranmer said.

"And anyway, I was taking care of him."

"His wife young, or what?"

"Younger than he. I think she's forty-three or so. Claims to be thirty-eight."

Cranmer grinned. "Good-looking?"

"If you like them like that. Heavy on the make-up and the hair spray. Art said she was very conservative in bed."

"Meaning what?"

"Mainly, no blow jobs," Tracy said.

Cranmer couldn't help staring at Tracy's mouth and wondering. The tip of her tongue peeked out, but he couldn't swear it was intentional. This is one outspoken lady, he thought.

"I'll go see the widow after I talk to the law," Cranmer said. "Say, I noticed Taber's jewelry store this morning. Sign on the outside says Taber and Rope. Who's Rope?"

"Art's partner," Tracy said. "Actually, Michael was here first, but not doing much business. Art bought in when he came to Solano from Ponca City."

"How long ago was that?"

"Seven years or so. Art really built up the business. I guess he was always a little cantankerous, but he can do wonderful things with jewels."

Tracy looked at her watch and stood up. Cranmer was very aware of her breasts stretching a pink sweater.

"Back to work," she said.

Cranmer rose and grabbed his cane.

"What's wrong with your leg?" Tracy asked.

"I smashed it," Cranmer said. "I was in a train that derailed. One of the seats came loose and landed on my leg."

Tracy picked up her purse. "Say, your assistant called me last night. Are you sure he's working?"

"There's a fifty percent chance." Cranmer laughed. "Why?"

"I'm sure he was drunk," Tracy said. "He woke me up about

two in the morning. Called me Aunt Tracy and told me he'd found a place to stay and not to worry about him. There was a lot of noise in the background."

"Just part of his cover," Cranmer explained. "Butch will know more about Solano than you do in a week. I don't see how he does it, but he's a master at insinuating himself into a town's confidence. He's a booze hound, and that helps."

"Well, I wish he'd let me get some sleep," Tracy said.

"He have any news for me?" Cranmer asked.

"No. He was just being a dutiful nephew."

"Okay," Cranmer said. "I'll go see the law and the widow and check you later."

He watched Tracy's hips appreciatively as she walked to her car.

The road crew was repairing a bridge which had washed out on a section-line road. Maneri didn't actually consider it a bridge, but that was what they called it. It just looked like a bump in the road to him.

Maneri had pulled out all the stops the night before, and he had quickly established the reputation as the best pool shooter to hit Solano in years. Normally Maneri was a hustler, missing shots purposely to string the suckers along, but he had shot his absolute best the previous night. He wanted to become known quickly—and he had succeeded.

He'd learned a good deal about Solano's politics but nothing of substance about Art Taber. He was handicapped because he wanted to wait until someone else brought up the subject.

Maneri stopped spreading asphalt to watch the approach of a white MG. It stopped a few yards up the road from the bridge, and the driver got out and walked up to the crew. He had a 35-mm. camera strapped around his neck.

Jerry Blefary shook hands with him and said, "Hi, Don."

Maneri wandered over to get in on the action.

Blefary made introductions. The newcomer was Donald Dorne, a reporter for the *Medwick Herald.* Dorne shot a few pictures of the road crew at work. Maneri engaged him in a conversation about photography. He remembered Dorne was the man who wrote the story about Solano's grant problems, and he figured if he was a typical reporter he'd be glad to talk about it. Still, the problem was how to introduce the subject.

Maneri gained some time by hitching a ride into Solano with Dorne. McIntosh Johnson had told him he could take the afternoon off to search for a place to stay. Maneri was about to use Jerry Blefary's pickup, but he decided to take advantage of the reporter's presence.

Dorne's bushy red hair made him resemble Art Garfunkel. He drove the MG as if there were no tomorrow.

Maneri sounded him out about a place to rent and hit an unexpected jackpot. "People don't usually have too much luck through the real estate agencies," Dorne said, "but I know one private landlord who owns half the rent houses in Solano. Name's Taber. Be careful when you go see her, though. Her husband just cut his throat, and she may be a shade irritable."

"Is that Art Taber?" Maneri asked.

Dorne nodded.

"Say, that rings a bell," Maneri said. "I remember now. I've read one of your stories. Something about Taber and a federal grant."

"Thought you just got to town," Dorne said.

"Yeah, dad, but Jerry had an old paper at his pad. I used it for a pillow."

"Well, that beats cat shit," said Dorne.

"Let me ask you a question," Maneri said. "I don't know much about newspapers, but I heard some people talking last night. Something about a cat that unlocks doors and was hooked into the suicide somehow. Seemed to me it'd make a hell of a story. But I haven't seen anything in the papers about it."

"Hell, that's just a hustle they're putting out," Dorne said. "Taber had a big old black cat named Orestes. There was some confusion over whether or not the bathroom door where Taber did the dirty deed was locked. His mistress found him, and she said the door was locked at first, then when she came back from checking out his car, it was open. So the law decided the cat opened it."

Maneri said quickly, "I thought Tracy Zantell found him."

"Yeah, that's right."

"You say she was his mistress?"

"Yeah."

"She's my aunt," Maneri said.

Dorne grunted. "I got a big mouth," he said.

"No problem," said Maneri. "She hadn't said anything to me about it. I guess she wants to keep it quiet. That cat fable sounds like a crock of shit to me."

"Me too. If I had my way, I'd blast it all over page one. But my editor is a cautious man. We played it way down."

"Guy sure died at a convenient time," Maneri said.

"Yeah. Makes you wonder, don't it?"

Dorne braked the MG to a halt in Solano's business section. Maneri thanked him for the lift and offered to buy him a drink that evening.

Dorne was amenable. "Got to hustle my big photographic scoop on the road gang back to the office. Let's meet at the motel about seven. You know where their club is?"

Maneri said yes and see you later.

Dorne goosed the MG, careened around a corner and disappeared.

While Maneri was debating whether to call Denise Taber or go see her about lodging, he noticed he was standing in front of Taber's jewelry store. He decided to test the water.

The salesgirl had a slender model's figure. She was alone in the store. She looked at Maneri's black jeans and black sweatshirt and said, "The man in black."

Maneri immediately assumed a fencing position and said, "My name is Inigo Montoya of Spain. You killed my father. Prepare to die."

The girl laughed delightedly. "You forgot your six-fingered sword," she said.

Maneri leaned on the counter and smiled at her. "I can't believe it," he said. "An oasis in the desert."

"I loved that book," she said. "You're the first person I've met who's read it."

"I'm a simple romantic," Maneri said. "I read Goldman and sip white wine. The men I work with told me Princess Buttercup, the most beautiful woman in the world, worked at the jewelry store. I'm convinced."

"It's Princess Martha," she said.

"I'm Butch Maneri."

"Martha Henning."

They shook hands formally. Maneri held onto her hand and said, "Will you marry me?"

She grinned at him.

"No? Well, then, will you go out with me?" He rotated her hand in his and saw no ring.

"Go out where?" she asked.

He shrugged. "We could scale the Cliffs of Insanity in the moonlight. I just got here. I don't know where to take you. I'm open to suggestions."

"Where are you from?" she asked.

"Tulsa," Maneri said. He had lived there once.

"What are you doing in Solano?"

"Working on the roads for the county."

She arched a painted eyebrow. "You're kidding."

"It's good honest work," Maneri said aloofly. "The main thing is I need some money. I've known McIntosh Johnson a long time, and he offered to help me escape destitution. Don't tell me you've worked around diamonds so long you've lost the flair for simplicity."

"Do you always yammer so much?"

"I'm nervous. I'm afraid if I stop talking, you'll say no," Maneri said seriously.

She smiled at him. "Oh, it's yes," she said. "It's only a question of working out the details."

"We could compare copies of *The Princess Bride.*"

"How about going to a club in Medwick?" Martha suggested. "I know a quiet place where we can talk and get to know each other."

"You mean there's nothing in Solano?"

"It's pretty slow here."

Maneri shook his head. "That's a problem, then," he said. "Provincial as it sounds, I don't have a car."

"No car? How do you get around?"

"Well, I hitchhiked into Solano. I just got here yesterday. Last night I stayed with Jerry Blefary. I've got the afternoon off to look for a place to live. I rode into town with some newspaper reporter."

"I went to school with Jerry," she said.

Maneri nodded. "You wouldn't want to share a house with me and save rent, would you?"

"I already have a house."

"Have room for a homeless waif? Skip it. What about tonight? I don't know if I can borrow a car or not. Why don't you drive? I assume if you have a house, you also have a car."

She shook her head. "I don't know why, but all right. But you're certainly getting off to an inauspicious beginning."

"I'll be at that club in the motel," Maneri said. "About eight?"

"All right."

Maneri gave her his best smile and left the store. Even if Denise Taber threw him out on his ear, the day would be a success.

Cranmer looked at the photograph sourly. It showed Art Taber's body lying halfway into a shower stall. The stall and Taber's shirt were spotted with what Cranmer took to be blood. Taber was lying face down, and his body was partially supported by his knees.

Cranmer looked at a second photograph. This one was a wide-angle shot of Taber's throat. The wound was just a big gash to Cranmer. He could make nothing out of it.

He looked at the first picture again and concentrated on the straight razor lying in the shower stall. The razor's position seemed consistent with the theory that Taber had sliced his own throat and then dropped the razor involuntarily.

"What's this stuff on the wall?" Cranmer asked.

Jamie Darden, Solano's city marshal, took the picture from Cranmer. "Blood," he said scornfully.

"Here on the wall?"

"Yeah, that's right."

Cranmer scratched his nose. "You figure he crouched down into the shower, slashed—and then fell forward?"

"That's how it reads," said Darden.

Cranmer watched the marshal thoughtfully. Darden was forty years old, he estimated, and had a large red nose which indicated he liked the juice of the grape. Cranmer wondered how a man managed to rise to the lofty position of Solano city marshal.

Dedication and valor, he decided.

Darden dressed to fit the part. He wore tight brown corduroy breeches with the cuffs stuffed into shiny brown cowboy boots. His shirt was a western affair with snaps, bright pink. He wore a holster strapped around his waist. It held a monstrous .45. His cowboy hat was white and huge. People could see him coming for miles, Cranmer thought.

"How do you figure the blood got over to the wall if he was in the shower?" Cranmer asked.

Darden shrugged. "Splashed," he said.

Cranmer looked at the picture skeptically.

"It's just like slaughterin' a steer," Darden said. "Blood don't always go where you want it to. Man cain't help it."

"Seems like a lot to splash," Cranmer demurred.

"Nah. Stuff spurts out faster than a man pissin' out fourteen beers."

Cranmer smiled unconsciously. "Tell me about this cat," he said.

"Nothin' much to tell. Woman says the bathroom door's locked when she gets there and then opens up by itself. Hell, everybody in town knows the Tabers got this foreign-named cat what can open the door. Used to show it off at parties. I seen it myself. Damn cat could go in the circus."

"Any blood on the cat?"

"None found."

"Seems if blood was spurting all over the bathroom and the cat was in there, it'd get splashed."

"Blood does funny things," said Darden.

Cranmer shook his head. "Well, I'll go see the widow. Thanks for the help."

"Nothin' to it."

Cranmer hoisted himself to his feet and limped toward the door.

"Say, how'd you bung up the leg?" Darden asked.

"Fell off a bull in a rodeo," Cranmer said.

Darden pulled his hat down over his eyes.

. . .

Denise Taber did a lot for black. Cranmer had just run through his pitch about the routine investigation of suicides. He leaned back in his chair and waited for the response. The widow looked at him with clear hazel eyes and said, "I'll be glad to help in any way I can. But the authorities seem certain about what happened."

"Well, there's a few things that don't fit. For instance, this business with the cat. Now, I'm having a hard time selling that to my supervisor."

"Would you like a demonstration?" Denise asked.

She didn't sound like she was talking about a cat, but Cranmer chalked that up to wishful thinking. She was older than Tracy Zantell, but she had breasts a man could kiss for an hour without touching the same spot twice.

"Sure," Cranmer said.

She led him up the stairs. Cranmer fought down an erection. Christ, he thought, these women are really getting to me today.

The cat was sleeping on the bed. She picked him up, petted him and carried him to the bathroom. Cranmer looked around the room he had seen in the pictures. He had a brief fantasy about throwing Denise Taber into the shower and raping her in the memory of her husband's blood.

"The door locks so," she said, pushing the knob in and rotating it. "Now we'll pull it shut and leave Orestes inside."

She closed the door and they went back downstairs.

Within two minutes Orestes joined them. Denise tossed him some candy from a dish on the coffee table. Orestes arched his back, purred and looked proud.

"Satisfied?" Denise said.

Cranmer grunted. He didn't like cats. Much less cats who opened doors. "Where were you when it happened?" he asked.

"In Oklahoma City, shopping."

"Alone?"

"Yes. I go up twice a week."

"What about this other woman, Tracy Zantell, who found the body? What was she doing here?"

Denise shrugged, creating interesting vibrations. "I'm sure I don't know," she said haughtily.

"Is it possible she and your husband had a thing going?"

"I would hope he had better taste."

The women don't like each other, Cranmer thought.

He pretended to get some information from his notebook. "This marshal, Jamie Darden, says the Zantell woman said she was here visiting," he said. "Does that fit in? Did she visit here often?"

"Occasionally."

"All right. Did your husband always use a straight razor?"

"Every day."

"That's an odd habit," Cranmer observed.

"He was old-fashioned."

Cranmer had run out of questions. He'd gotten more information from certain rocks he could recall.

He stood up, leaned on his cane and recited thanks. He accidentally wandered into the study on his way out. As he peered casually at some papers on the desk, Denise Taber followed him into the room. "Did you bring a warrant for a search, Mr. Cranmer?" she asked icily.

Cranmer grinned and said, "No, ma'am." He left the house wondering what secret the study might contain.

Cranmer roamed the neighborhood for two hours after leaving Denise Taber. From what he could ascertain, the same people were home on this Wednesday afternoon that had been home the previous Thursday. Mostly it was housewives. They added little to Cranmer's data bank. Nobody had seen anything unusual. He got the idea they spent their time glued to television sets, impervious to the outside world.

Following another fruitless interview, Cranmer left the last house which had a view of the Taber residence. He was going down the walk to the street when suddenly a small girl in a yellow dress appeared before him.

"Hi, mister." Her voice was surprisingly deep.

Nodding absently, Cranmer kept going.

"Have you been with my mother?"

He sighed and stopped walking. "If your mother's the woman in that house, yes."

"Sure she is. I'm Melissa."

"Figures." Cranmer did not like children. One of his favorite quotes was W. C. Fields' statement that he liked to hear children cry because that meant someone might come and take them away.

"Where's your car?" Melissa demanded.

He spread his hands.

"You really should have a car. A black car, because they're the best. Nobody walks any more," she said sagely.

He shrugged. They faced each other across the sidewalk. "How did you hurt your foot?" said Melissa.

Which focused Cranmer's attention on his throbbing knee. "Whatever turns you on, kid," he said and began walking off.

"Were you in a car wreck?"

He sighed again. "That's what. A car wreck. I used to drive race cars, and I crashed into the wall at the fourth turn at Indianapolis."

"The 500," Melissa said firmly. "Did you know Mario Andretti? He's my favorite racer."

"That's good news. Why? Does he drive a black car?"

"No, the black car parks out in front of our house. The man just sits in his black car and lets me look at it."

Cranmer started paying attention. "Who's the man?" he asked.

"I don't know."

"When did you see him last?"

"Thursday. I know because that's the first day I was sick. I've been sick a week."

"You don't act sick. What did the man look like?"

"I don't know. He has some kind of an eagle or something on his forehead."

Cranmer resisted the impulse to smack her with his cane. "Do you know what kind of car it is?"

"A black one."

"Yeah. But is it a Ford, a Chevrolet, or what?"

"Well, it's the one with the metal spare tire in back. Lincoln. Did you know Lincoln and Kennedy repeated history?"

"What time Thursday?"

"Melissa!"

Cranmer and the girl both spun around. The woman Cranmer

had just interviewed stood in the doorway, screaming, "Get in this house! Now!"

Melissa smiled at Cranmer. "Bye," she said.

Cranmer nodded vaguely at her. Once Melissa was safely inside the house, the mother came storming out after Cranmer. "What do you think you're doing? Trying to intimidate a little . . ."

"Oh, fuck off, lady," said Cranmer.

The woman gasped and ran back toward the house. Laughing, Cranmer started limping down the street.

He felt better than he had in weeks.

Richard Straight hung up the telephone and said to Coady, "We've got a make."

"About time," Coady said. "Do we move?"

"That's what they say. I think it's a bad idea."

"Why?"

"Look, we know the guy saw us, right? But he hasn't told anybody about it. As far as I can tell, everyone's buying the suicide angle. Now, the only reason for this character to keep mum is that he doesn't want to admit he was there. I can't imagine why, but I never argue with luck. If we lean on the guy, we may change his mind about talking. It may be worth a hassle to him if he finds out we're wise to him. I think we ought to leave well enough alone."

Coady shrugged. "How do you know the guy won't change his mind?"

"I don't. It simply doesn't make sense to me to pressure somebody who's being quiet into being quiet."

Coady began popping his knuckles one at a time. "But the orders are to go see him?"

Straight nodded. "So we'll go see him. Heaven forbid we should ignore an order because it's nonsense." He set a pan of water on the hot plate.

Maneri let Dorne buy the second round.

"Man, you move fast," said the newspaper reporter. "That Martha Henning fills the dreams of many a lowly peasant."

"I fit the qualifications," Maneri said. "Say, thanks for the steer on the Taber woman. I now have a home."

"You go see her?"

"Yeah. She's a nice-looking woman. All business, though. I thought maybe with her husband out of the way, she'd be looking for action. No such luck."

"I doubt she's wasting away," said Dorne. "Looks like I'm not the only one who's skeptical about Taber's suicide."

"Meaning?"

"There's an insurance investigator in town. Guy named Cranmer. He's been roaming around asking questions. The mayor told me about him. I think I'll try for an interview—if I can convince my editor."

Maneri grinned. One of the members of the road crew yelled at Maneri from the pool table, "Hey, Butch! Come shoot some partners."

Maneri checked the time and passed it up.

Dorne said, "How did you get thick with these people so soon? I've been covering this beat for over a year, and they're just now getting to where they'll talk to me."

Maneri shrugged. "I work with them."

"Yeah," said Dorne. "But you don't work with Martha Henning."

"I'd like to," said Maneri.

Dorne pulled a parlay card out of his shirt pocket. "You play these things?" he asked.

"Compulsively," said Maneri. He took the card and looked it over. "Looks like some easy money," he said. "Air Force only giving Navy six points; Texas ten to Arkansas; and check these last four: Maryland, Michigan, Ohio State and Penn State. That's a good four-team parlay right there. You take the bets on these?"

"I can place 'em for you," Dorne said.

"You bet parlays or straight?" Maneri asked.

"Usually three teamers," Dorne said. "I don't win much."

"Hell, that's the joy of a parlay," Maneri said. "All you have to do is hit one and you're set for the season."

Martha Henning walked into the club. She was wearing a simple red dress. Maneri still thought she looked like a model.

He stood up and pulled out a chair. "Hello, Buttercup," he said. "You know Don Dorne?"

She nodded and sat down.

"Let me finish a business transaction and we'll go," said Maneri. He gave Dorne a twenty. "Put this on the last four teams," he instructed.

"You're giving away a lot of points."

"Yeah, well, I like to play these things fast, before I have time to think. Thinking always louses me up."

Dorne laughed and filled out the card.

Maneri took his stub and said, "Let's go to Medwick, sweet lady. Later, Donald."

Maneri drove Martha's Mustang to Medwick. He parked next to a black Lincoln Continental at the Colonial Club.

"Looks like my boss is here," said Martha.

"Huh?" Maneri said brilliantly. "I don't want to stick my foot in my mouth, but I heard your boss was dead."

"That's Art Taber," she said. "He killed himself. The Lincoln belongs to my other boss, Mr. Rope. He and Mr. Taber were partners."

Maneri took her arm and steered her into the club. Tracy Zantell was sitting at a table with a graying man.

"There's my aunt," said Maneri.

"There's Mr. Rope," said Martha.

They walked over to the table. "Hello, Aunt Tracy," said Maneri. "Didn't know you frequented these low-class joints."

"Hi, Butch," Tracy said. "Hello, Martha. Butch, this is Michael Rope. Mike, my nephew, Butch Maneri."

The two men shook hands. Maneri and Martha joined the other couple.

Rope insisted on buying drinks. "You didn't say anything about a nephew, Tracy," he said. "Been in town long?"

"Drifted in yesterday," Maneri said.

The quartet conversed politely for a while, then Rope and Tracy rose to leave. Maneri wrote down his address and phone number and handed them to Tracy. "I like for people to know how to get in touch with me," he said.

Tracy nodded, indicating she would inform Cranmer.

Rope was being jovial. He told Maneri and Martha they could

drink out of his bottle. "Just you be sure to let her get some sleep tonight," he told Maneri. "She's an invaluable employee when she's sober."

Maneri muttered an appropriate response and watched them leave. "I've got a good-looking aunt, huh?" he said.

"I didn't know you had relatives in Solano."

"We've never been real close," Maneri said honestly.

The Colonial, as advertised, was quiet. A woman with a soft voice played at the piano bar. Maneri and Martha traded getting-to-know-you information.

A man called Buster who had been at the motel the previous night came to the table and spoke to Maneri. He turned down the offer of a drink because he was gambling on the pool table. When he departed, Martha said, "Did you know these people before or did you meet them all in one day?"

"One day," said Maneri. "I was shooting pool with Buster last night. I think he likes me because I didn't try to hustle him. He shoots fair, but I could have taken him for a bundle."

"You don't seem the type to hang around bars and shoot pool," Martha said.

"Well, appearances are deceiving."

They drank Rope's whiskey till just before midnight. Maneri danced with Martha several times. As the night progressed, they danced slower and slower and closer and closer.

"That's the only thing cowboy music is good for," Maneri said. "You can dance slow to it and ignore the words."

"I don't mind western music," Martha said. "I wouldn't buy any of it, but it's all you can hear around here. I guess I developed a taste for it in self-defense."

Maneri paid the tab. He still hadn't kissed her. He'd learned quite a bit about the jewelry operation, but nothing startling.

As he was holding the door open for Martha, he heard her say, "Clark!" Then a fist exploded in his face.

Maneri went down. When he looked up, he saw Martha screaming at a bulky man with a crew cut. He felt a wild surge of joy. Buster came to the door with a cue stick in his hand. "What goes?" he asked.

"I haven't worked it out yet," Maneri said, grinning.

"I'm gonna teach this long-haired freak to fuck around with my girl," Clark said.

Buster hefted the cue stick. Martha started railing at Clark again.

"Cool it," Maneri said. "If he wants me, he can have me. Buster, keep him off me till I get up."

Maneri put his hand on his lip and felt blood trickling. Not wanting to get his velour sweater bloody he pulled it over his head as he slowly stood up. His pale body glistened in the neon light. He flexed his shoulder muscles happily. He figured he was giving away forty pounds.

Most of the occupants of the club had come out to watch the action. Maneri handed his sweater to Martha. He shook his head sadly. "I didn't notice you wearing a ring," he said without rancor.

"I don't," Martha said. "This low life thinks . . ."

"You're kidding," Maneri interrupted. "This clown doesn't really know how to think, does he?"

Clark swung at Maneri. Maneri ducked and stepped out into the parking lot where he'd have room to maneuver. Clark came after him. The onlookers tensed.

Maneri stepped inside the next wild swing and clubbed Clark's stomach. Clark gasped a bit and tried to grab Maneri, but Maneri was already out of reach. He laughed at Clark. "Come on, friend," he sneered. "Hit me while I'm looking at you."

Clark charged. Maneri danced aside and slapped the side of his head as he went by.

Clark reversed his field and came again. This time Maneri stood his ground. When Clark was in range, he kicked him in the stomach. Clark doubled over. Maneri gave him a minute to recover. Clark panted and charged again. Maneri tripped him.

Clark tried to get up and Maneri kicked him in the face. He felt the face give beneath his shoe. He stepped back and grinned. "Get up and cut my hair, friend," he said.

"Please, Butch," Martha pleaded. "Let's go."

Clark stood up. Blood ran down his face. He had a knife in his hand.

The sight of the knife accentuated the savage glow inside Maneri. "Buster!" he called in a voice totally without tension. He held out his hand and Buster tossed him the pool cue. Maneri held the cue stick casually by his side. "Come on, friend," he said to Clark.

Clark, bleeding and panting, glared at Maneri for a long moment. Then his nerve broke. He turned and walked off.

Maneri laughed mirthlessly. The tension in the crowd snapped and an excited yammering broke out. Maneri heard Buster explaining what had happened and who Maneri was.

Maneri handed the pool cue to Buster, winked his thanks and walked over to Martha. He wiped his face and shrugged into his shirt. "Sorry about that," he said carelessly to Martha.

She touched his lip gently. "You couldn't help it." Her voice was tremulous. She gestured to the crowd. "You're going to have quite a reputation by tomorrow."

"It's the rest of tonight I'm interested in," Maneri said.

They walked to the car. Before he started the engine Maneri got his first kiss. His cut lip didn't bother him at all.

Maneri's stomach was throbbing. The fight had stirred him up, and Martha had failed to cool him off. She claimed the battle had upset her too much.

Maneri didn't push her. He was a patient man. He drank a glass of milk, smoked a joint and started walking the streets of Solano. It was 1:30 A.M. when he came to Tracy Zantell's house. No black Lincoln was in evidence, so he knocked on the front door. After a few minutes Tracy answered the door. She was wearing a diaphanous nightgown.

"Hello, Auntie," Maneri said.

"Jesus Christ," said Tracy. "Don't you ever sleep? Or let anyone else sleep?"

They went into the house. Maneri was slightly stoned. "Where's the executive?" he asked.

"Oh, he left in a huff. I told him I'd hired someone to investigate Art's death. It upset him."

"Yeah? Did you tell him who?"

"No. It really sort of slipped out."

"Pillow talk, huh?"

"No. We hadn't got that far yet, if it's any concern of yours."

"Just looking out for my aunt," Maneri said. "You know, you really shouldn't let things slip out. It can be very frustrating."

Tracy considered the various meanings of that statement. She by-passed it and said, "What happened to your lip?"

"I made a pass at Martha and she scratched it."

Tracy shook her head. "I've got an incorrigible nephew," she said sadly.

"Nah," Maneri said, "I'm just horny." He stood up. "Guess I'd better get out of your hair."

Tracy stretched and yawned. She could feel Maneri's eyes follow the movement of her breasts. She said, "I'm horny too."

Maneri grinned delightedly. "I like a lady who speaks her mind," he said. He stepped over to her and ran his hands over her body.

"You've certainly got more energy than your boss," she murmured. "He acts like he's in a trance."

"He usually is," said Maneri. "Where's the bed? I've never fucked an aunt before."

Tracy sighed and slipped off the nightgown. "I'll see if I can narrow the generation gap," she said.

Maneri's eyes gleamed like a cat's.

Maneri rapped on Cranmer's door at 4 A.M. Thursday. Cranmer opened his eyes groggily and peered around the motel room. The lights from outside pierced the curtains as if they weren't there. The room glowed.

Maneri hit the door again. Cranmer rolled out of bed, limped to the door and called, "Who?"

"Young Maneri," Maneri said softly.

Cranmer scowled and opened the door.

Maneri displayed two paper cups filled with coffee. "I come bearing gifts, O Great One," he said.

"Terrific," muttered Cranmer. He left Maneri standing in the doorway and went into the bathroom to take some Demerol. When he emerged, Maneri was sitting in the room's single chair.

"What the hell are you doing prowling around?" Cranmer demanded.

Maneri handed him a coffee cup. "Have some elixir," he said. "I've been servicing our client."

Cranmer sat on the edge of the bed and rubbed his eyes. He said, "Meaning?"

"Fucking."

"Zantell?"

"That's who."

Cranmer shook his head. "Don't give me any details," he said. "I couldn't stand it."

Maneri removed two cardboard containers of cream from his shirt pocket. He ripped off the tops and sucked out the cream.

"That's supposed to go in coffee," Cranmer said.

"I have to protect my stomach. Say, this is an active little burg, huh?"

"I hadn't noticed it," Cranmer said sourly.

"You must be going to the wrong places. Learned anything dramatic yet?"

"Nah." Cranmer poured half his coffee out of the cup and replaced it with bourbon. "You know anybody with an eagle tattooed on his forehead?"

"Just my great aunt, and she had it removed surgically."

Cranmer told him about the little girl's vision.

Maneri grinned. "Well, pay my salary," he drawled. "I found the Lincoln for you, and I didn't even know I was looking for it."

"That's one of your rare talents," Cranmer said dryly.

"Man named Rope," Maneri said. "Ring any bells?"

"Taber's partner," said Cranmer. "I like it." He lit a Camel and scratched his nose. The pills were starting to act. "I've had a hard time buying the idea someone killed Taber because he wouldn't sell his business," he said. "Now, a partner snooping around raises several interesting possibilities. Maybe he was gouging the company. Trouble is, I didn't have a chance to ask the brat if the man in the black car ever got out of it."

"If she was busy playing, she might not have noticed," Maneri said. "But I've got an even better motive for you. It's always money or passion, right? So being a partner in the jewelry store gives Rope a possible money motive. Guess who he was with tonight?"

Cranmer just looked at him.

"My aunt," Maneri said. "The ubiquitous Tracy Zantell. She was shacked up with Taber, right? Taber croaks and Rope moves right in. And I guarantee it's impossible to have a platonic relationship with that woman."

"I like it," Cranmer said. "Say he suspects Zantell and Taber are dampening the sheets. He follows the broad, then—hell, what happens then? Whoever killed Taber had to be in the house before Zantell arrived."

"Still possible," Maneri said. "Maybe he'd followed her before and established the pattern. So he knows Taber gets there first. He arrives early, gets inside the house and exercises his slashing arm. But he miscalculates the timing and Tracy shows up before he can get out."

"How about this?" Cranmer said. "He cuts it fine because he wants Zantell to see her dead lover. Punishment of a sort. That would fit in with a jealousy kill."

Maneri finished his coffee and yawned. "It might not be Rope's Lincoln, though," he said. "Rope may have been in Zanzibar last Thursday."

"Well, we know he wasn't home," Cranmer said.

"Yeah? How?"

"Because Zantell told me she called him after she got worried and before she found the body. No answer. He told her later he was playing golf, but he could have been right behind her. Anyway, he was in town."

"Easy to check the golf story," Maneri said. "There's one other indication, for what it's worth. Tracy said she told Rope tonight she'd hired an investigator. It freaked him out. He stormed out of the house without even getting laid."

"Sounds good," Cranmer said.

"Want me to check the golf course tomorrow?" Maneri asked.

"No, I'll do it. I've got some traveling in mind for you. Tomorrow—today—is Thursday. I want you to finagle a car and follow this Denise Taber. She's supposed to go to the City and shop. Word is she goes there and shacks up. It might be helpful to know which is true. And if it's the second, who she's sleeping with."

Maneri nodded. "I can get wheels all right," he said. "Do you know when she leaves?"

"Stake her out," Cranmer said. "Get the car, then come get me and I'll wait with you. I want to hit the house while she's gone. She got snotty with me when I started roaming around this afternoon. Could be she's hiding something." He told Maneri about his aborted visit to the study.

"I'd like to visit her bedroom," Maneri said. "Seems like the middle-aged broads in this village are something else."

"Where did you run into the widow?" Cranmer asked.

"Hell, dad, she's my landlady. If you cared about my welfare, you'd have asked me by now if I found a place to stay."

"I have faith in you," Cranmer said. "You mean she's your landlady and you haven't gotten into her pants yet? You're slipping."

Maneri shrugged. "She's a very businesslike landlady. Didn't Tracy give you my address and phone number?"

Cranmer shook his head. Maneri gave him the information. Cranmer closed his eyes and felt the room drift around him.

"Hey, dad," Maneri said. Cranmer opened his eyes. "Don't pass out. I've got more news. A newspaper reporter's wise to you. Sort of. He thinks you're an insurance investigator. Said he's going to try to interview you. He thinks Taber was murdered."

"Seems to be a popular surmise," Cranmer said. He filled his coffee cup with bourbon and sipped it.

"I almost forgot the most important thing," Maneri said. "Did you get the lines on the football games?"

Cranmer grinned at him. "Yeah, I called Wally."

"What'd you bet?"

"Haven't placed them yet. Got to analyze the spreads."

Maneri told him about his four-team parlay. Cranmer shook his head sadly. "I keep telling you, Butch, straight bets are the only way to make money."

"Not enough excitement," Maneri said.

"Who cares about excitement?" Cranmer said. "It's winning money that counts. I've pretty much decided to go with Air Force, Texas and Tennessee."

"Tennessee? How many points are you getting?"

"Alabama's giving fifteen on a straight bet. I don't think they can beat Tennessee that much."

"That's what you thought about Michigan and Michigan State," Maneri reminded him.

Cranmer shrugged. "There's no sure bets."

Maneri stood up. "I'd better go line up some wheels and get the day off," he said. "You'll cry when I win two hundred dollars on my parlay and you lose your ass being conservative."

"Yeah," said Cranmer. "Come get me when you get the car, and we'll eat some breakfast."

"Right on, dad," Maneri said exuberantly. "Far out."

Cranmer winced.

Four

A wasp buzzed against the back window of Jerry Blefary's pickup. Maneri jumped and hunched his shoulders. "Goddamn thing," he said.

Cranmer laughed at him. "Ignore it," he said. "It's cold. It won't bother you."

Maneri watched the wasp climb up the window. He shivered and got out of the truck. "Kill the son of a bitch," he told Cranmer.

Cranmer shook his head. "You've got some weird fears, young Maneri," he said. He reached back and crushed the wasp with his left thumb. The wasp arched its back and plunged its stinger into Cranmer's thumb. He didn't seem to notice. When the wasp stopped moving, he flipped it out the window.

"All right, Butch," he said condescendingly, "it's safe now."

Maneri climbed back into the truck. "Those things make me nervous," he said.

The pickup was parked two blocks from the Taber house. The house itself was not visible, but they could see the point where the driveway met the street.

"I think I'll buy another car," Maneri said.

"What's wrong with the Fiat?"

"Oh, I'll keep it. But I need a car I can use on jobs. The Fiat's too damned distinctive. I think I'll buy an old Ford or Chevrolet for tailing people. It's a pain having to borrow wheels all the time."

"I've been doing it for years," Cranmer said.

"Yeah, but you're a pain anyway, so it evens out."

It was ten o'clock before Denise Taber left. Maneri punched Cranmer, who had fallen asleep. "Rise and shine, dad."

Cranmer stepped out of the pickup. "Don't go to sleep on the road," he said.

Maneri grinned. "Not to worry. I ate some Dexamyl before I picked you up. I'm good for the rest of the day and the night."

Maneri chugged after Denise Taber. Cranmer rubbed the sleep out of his eyes and limped up to the Taber house. He didn't notice anyone watching him.

The front door was no problem. Cranmer had a good set of keys, and he was inside as quickly as if it were his own home. He went through the house speedily and thoroughly.

The desk in the study held the only material of interest. Cranmer perused a file of canceled checks, then copied some information into his notebook. One drawer in the desk was locked. He took out a straight piece of metal the size of a large needle and picked the lock. The drawer was empty.

Cranmer scratched his nose and thought about it. Why lock an empty drawer? He couldn't come up with a reasonable answer.

He went through the trash without finding anything, then hobbled up the stairs to the bathroom where Art Taber had died. It looked exactly as it had the day before. Cranmer scowled, sat on the stool and lit a Camel.

Orestes came into the bathroom and rubbed against Cranmer's legs. He petted the cat absently. Then he stood up abruptly and locked the bathroom door. "Open it, cat," he said.

Orestes jumped on the stool daintily, curled up and started purring. Cranmer eased down to the floor. Feeling idiotic, he lay on his back with his shoulders and head in the shower stall.

The black cat jumped down to the floor and walked over and licked Cranmer's face. Cranmer tried to conceal his revulsion. He pretended he was dead.

Open the door, cat, he thought.

Cranmer lay on the bathroom floor for half an hour. After a while Orestes returned to his perch on the stool. The cat went to sleep. Cranmer glared at Orestes. Finally he hoisted himself to his feet and went back downstairs. Orestes accompanied him.

Maybe it would be different if I was covered with blood, Cranmer thought.

He left the house with a strong feeling of discontent.

Denise Taber drove on the freeway, and tailing her was a simple matter. But Maneri's stomach was churning. No sleep, the booze, the fight, the upper were all working against him. He figured the Dexamyl was doing the most damage. Unconsciously he ground his teeth as he drove along.

He shifted position occasionally, mostly out of habit, because Denise Taber was paying no attention to the traffic. Maneri led her for a while, then dropped behind and followed her. Luckily he was behind her when she took the Robinson Street exit into Norman.

Maneri followed her along Robinson past the airport, then up Berry. She turned off Berry onto Canterbury and parked in front of a half-brick house. Maneri stopped and watched her walk into it. He gave her fifteen minutes, then he drove slowly past the house.

The name on the mailbox was Kilduff.

Maneri curved his way around the block and settled down to wait. He scrawled the house number in the dust on the dash. After an hour Maneri lit a joint and slouched down in the seat of the pickup. He felt as conspicuous as the fly in the soup. Two joints and three hours later he didn't care.

Denise Taber and a slender man of about thirty came out of the house. The man was carrying an armload of packages. The shopping trip, Maneri thought. He couldn't make out any labels, but he assumed the boxes were from Oklahoma City stores.

Denise Taber drove straight home. Maneri drifted along behind her, making no effort to conceal his presence. He enjoyed the trip.

Richard Straight glanced at his watch, then closed his book and placed it on the floor by his chair. He downed the dregs of his boiled water. "It's time, Ham," he said.

Hamilton Coady turned off *The Price Is Right.* "Wonder how much that trip to Hawaii costs?" he said.

Straight ignored him and checked the action of his .45 Colt.

"Gonna carry heat this time?" Coady asked.

"Might help frighten him," Straight said.

"I still don't see why we don't just waste the dude," Coady complained.

Straight shoved the Colt into its holster, snapped the holster onto his belt and shrugged into a greenish-plaid sports jacket. "If we kill another guy, it weakens the suicide theory," he said patiently. "Even hick law will catch on if half the town starts falling over dead."

Coady popped a knuckle, then stuck it in his mouth and sucked on it. "Let's drift," he said.

They left the room and retrieved their rented car from the hotel garage. At Straight's instruction, Coady had traded the LTD for an Impala. Coady sat behind the wheel and carefully strapped himself into place with seat belt and shoulder harness. Straight eyed the safety precautions impassively, then slouched in the passenger seat and ignited a cigarette.

Coady made the trip from Medwick to Solano without violating any traffic regulations. Straight whistled the theme from the first movement of Tchaikovsky's *Pathétique.* Finally Coady glared at him and pointedly turned on the radio. Jim Croce began singing about LeRoy Brown. Coady tapped his fingers on the steering wheel in time to the music.

"You know you're listening to a dead man?" Straight asked.

Coady glanced at him blankly.

"That singer went down with a plane a while back," said Straight. "Must be odd for his family to listen to him sing."

Coady shrugged. "It's a good song," he said.

Straight sighed and looked out the window. Temperatures were dropping, but it was still warm for October. The leaves on the trees were still green. They were also still on the trees. Straight's favorite season was autumn. If this was the best Oklahoma could do for autumn, he was glad he didn't live here.

Coady dodged the business section of Solano and parked the rented Chevrolet behind a small apartment complex. The apartments formed a semicircle which embraced a swimming pool. Half a dozen cars were parked in front. Coady had parked in the rear. A weedy, trash-strewn vacant lot separated them from the convex tip of the apartments.

It took Coady a full minute to extricate himself from the straps which imprisoned him. Straight waited patiently beside the car. The sun was on the wane, but the day was still bright.

Straight adjusted his auburn wig. It was designed to give him the mod look, but the hair straggling over his ears made him feel like a sack of potatoes infested with cockroaches. He resisted the temptation to shove the artificial hair back.

Coady joined him. "You and Howard Hunt, huh?" he said.

Straight looked at him blankly.

"You know," Coady said. "The CIA cat what set up the Watergate deal. It said on the news the CIA give him a wig for the job. I guess all you folks use the same tricks, huh?"

Straight reached into the back seat of the car and snared an attaché case. The case was packed with literature about the Encyclopaedia Britannica. If they stumbled into something unexpected, they would become encyclopedia salesmen.

Carrying the case in his left hand, Straight cautiously traversed the littered lot. He dodged a variety of empty beer cans, whiskey bottles, prophylactics, potato-chip bags, dog-food sacks and cans and neat piles of animal excrement. Luxury living in a modern apartment, he thought sardonically.

Coady waded through the refuse pachydermatously.

Michael Rope lived in an upstairs apartment. Straight and Coady climbed the stairs briskly and stopped before Rope's door. Straight rapped on the door while his eyes made a surreptitious survey of the surrounding apartments. He could see no motion. It was a quarter to five. They had timed it so they could make the entry before the apartment dwellers began to return home from work.

Straight removed the section of hard celluloid from his inside jacket pocket and leaned against the door. He tapped on the door with his left hand while his right forced open the latch. Then he called "All right, thanks" for the benefit of unseen neighbors and swung the door open. Hopefully, anyone watching would believe they had received verbal permission to enter.

Straight closed the door from the inside and locked it. "Keep an eye out," he told Coady.

Coady thumbed the drapes away from the picture window and gazed through the opening. Straight checked the apartment. It consisted of two large bedrooms, a built-in kitchen, living room, dining room and bath. Judging by the quality of the furniture, Straight assumed the apartment had come unfurnished. Rope had evidently invested a bundle in interior decorating.

The bed was unmade. Straight estimated there were over twenty-five suits in the walk-in closet. A man of sartorial resplendence, he thought ironically. The closet also contained a set of golf clubs in a fancy bag. Straight knew nothing of golf, but the equipment appeared expensive.

The second bedroom was more of a den. An enormous home entertainment center consumed one wall. Color television, phonograph, AM/FM radio and a tape player, all encased in walnut. A black and white couch against the opposite wall seemed a good prescription for eyestrain. Above the couch was an op-art painting in which black and white swirls of paint seemed to move. Straight shook his head, and felt the auburn wig shift with the motion. He stepped into the bathroom and gazed at his reflection in a mirror. His image returned his stare. Straight felt a strange sense of unease. If he had been anyone else, he might have considered it nerves. He chalked the feeling up to his discontent with the job in the offing.

He checked the time. Five of five. He removed an eyebrow pencil from his pants pocket and absently altered his features. He darkened the area beneath his eyes and added a few wrinkles to his cheeks. The black wrinkles looked unnatural, so he pulled a facial tissue from a slot in the wall and erased them. Then he smudged his darkened eye pouches. He dropped the used tissue in the stool and flushed it.

Straight returned to the living room. Coady was still staring insensibly through the window.

"Got the runs?" Coady asked without turning.

Straight said nothing. He sat in an easy chair and drummed his fingers against the arm.

"My kidneys used to act up during a job," Coady commented reminiscently. "I even pissed in my pants once. That was back when I first started. Back when I was still wasting people long-distance. It was the watching and waiting what always scratched at my kidneys."

Straight dug a long butt out of an ashtray and set fire to it.

"They's some cars comin' now," Coady said. "Goddamn, they's a couple of truly boxy broads getting out of that one. One with long blond hair's really putting on a show. That skirt ain't overlong anyhow, and, man, you oughta see her twist outa that car. It do make my mouth water."

Straight dragged deeply on the cigarette, made a face, peered at the brand name by the filter and mashed it out in the ashtray. The ashtray was round and white, with rippled sides. Straight figured it was supposed to represent a golf ball.

"Maybe he don't come straight home on Thursdays, Spinoza," Coady said. He interlaced his fingers and cracked his knuckles impatiently.

"He'll show," Straight said impassively. "Just a matter of when."

Coady pried open the drapes again. Straight began whistling Tchaikovsky softly. He directed an imaginary orchestra with the index finger of his right hand.

"Hey, Spinoza, I got a riddle for you," Coady said. "Think you can turn off that whistling long enough for a good riddle?"

Straight sighed. "Proceed, Plato," he said.

Coady rotated his head and stared hard at Straight for a moment. Then he looked back out the window and said, "There's three guys standing there naked. No clothes on, nothing in their hands. One's a nigger, one's an injun, and the other one's a white man. Now, can you figure out which one is the doctor?"

Straight allowed an appropriate amount of time to elapse before he said, "I give up."

"It's the nigger," Coady chortled. "He's the only one what's got his black bag."

Straight curled his lip. "Oh," he said tonelessly. He began tapping his fingers on the chair arm again.

Coady tensed by the window.

"Here comes the Lincoln," he said. "Man's all alone."

"Good," said Straight. "One problem eliminated already." He had been afraid Rope would bring company. The way this job—the thirteenth, he reminded himself—had been going, he had almost expected the witness to appear with a police escort.

"He's coming upstairs," Coady reported.

"Fine," said Straight. His tension had abated. "You go in the bedroom now," he instructed Coady. "Come out and let him see you right after I make the pitch."

Coady let the drapes fall back into place and tramped toward the bedroom. Straight walked across the living room and stood in the corner of the room behind the door. The open door would conceal him until Rope was inside.

A key scratched at the lock. The door swung open and the jeweler stepped into the apartment. He was carrying a bag of groceries. He left the door open, with keys dangling from the lock, and trudged into the kitchen with the groceries. Straight removed the keys and silently closed and locked the door. He turned to face Rope, who was coming back into the living room.

Rope's eyes gave him away before he had a chance to speak. His eyes reflected instant recognition and apprehension.

Straight tossed him the keys. Rope caught them unconsciously and shoved them in his pants pocket. His eyes made a quick circuit of the room, then met Straight's. The man with the graying crew cut appeared terrified.

"Well," Straight mused, "I don't have to ask if you know me. The question is what do you plan to do about it. Sit down, Mr. Rope. This shouldn't take much of your time."

Trancelike, Rope sat in the easy chair. Straight settled onto an overstuffed love seat. He let the silence build. He figured Rope's imagination could conjure much more vivid threats than any he could make verbally.

Straight started to scratch his left ear, then let it go. Why draw attention to the fact he was wearing a wig and it was uncomfortable?

"Got a smoke?" Straight asked Rope.

Rope extracted a gold cigarette case. He flipped a cigarette across to Straight. "Have one yourself," Straight suggested. Rope lit a cigarette and replaced the gold case. His movements were those of an automaton.

"You've given us some anxious moments, Mr. Rope," said Straight. He kept his voice free and light. "And I'll be honest with you: some people dislike anxiety, and when they ponder the possibilities of this situation they conclude their most viable option, so to speak, is to let you join Mr. Taber."

Rope's face paled a little more. His lips writhed, but no sound came out.

"Personally I don't agree with their thinking," Straight confided. "I see it this way. We know you saw us. You know you saw us. We all know you haven't said anything about it. Now, I have a high regard for trust, Mr. Rope. I wouldn't find it too difficult to trust you to remain silent. That is, I wouldn't find it overly straining if I knew what your motives are. Now, that's reasonable, isn't it? I'm perfectly willing to let the past sleep—if you can assure me you're not a walking alarm clock. Can you give me that assurance, Mr. Rope?"

Straight sucked on his cigarette and exhaled smoke in Rope's general direction.

Rope stuttered a little, then managed to say, "Listen, I'll do whatever you want. It was totally accidental. You've got to believe that. I certainly didn't mean to see you."

Straight watched Rope squirm, dispassionately. He took another leisurely puff on the cigarette, then leaned forward and stubbed it out. He watched the remnants of the smoke drift up to the ceiling. "I believe that, Mr. Rope," he said. "But that's not the motivation I'm talking about. Isn't it obvious it makes no difference whether you spotted us intentionally or not? What matters is you did see us. Now, why didn't you tell the law what you saw?"

Color returned to Rope's face. Given a healthy complexion, it might have been assumed he was blushing. "I was following the woman," he said. He actually hung his head. "I'm in love with her. I've craved her for years, but she never gave me a second glance. I had to know why. I'd heard some rumors about her and Art Taber, but I couldn't believe she'd actually prefer an old man to me. She lives alone; she runs her own business; she never seemed to go out. I was baffled. And it was tearing me apart. Her store's close to mine, so I saw her every day. Every day she looked better to me, and every day I wanted her more. So I followed her. I guess it was really sort of an excuse to be near her. I'd been following her for about a week when it happened."

Straight stared at him expressionlessly. It sounds like something a character who owns twenty-five suits would do, he thought. "Let's have another smoke," he said.

Rope distributed cigarettes. His frantic eyes could not meet Straight's calm gaze.

"Who's the woman?" Straight asked.

Rope hesitated.

"I'll give you a clue, friend," Straight said. He let some frost creep into his voice. "It was in the papers. I'm giving you the chance to come clean. If you value the continuation of your breathing, you won't try to dodge me."

"You won't hurt her, will you?" said Rope. "I'd rather sacrifice myself than hurt her."

"Very noble," Straight said. "Are you aware of some reason why we should bother the lady?"

"No, no, nothing like that," Rope blurted. "It's just that— Her name is Tracy Zantell. She's the one who found Art's body. I followed her from the time she closed her gift shop last Thursday. She drove to Taber's and parked in the back. I waited in the street because I knew she'd have to leave that way. The car you got into was already parked down the street from Taber's—down the opposite direction from where I was. I just sat there. I . . . I just . . . I don't know what you want me to say . . ."

Straight tapped the ash off his cigarette and scratched his ear. Then he dropped his hand irritably. "You followed the woman to Taber's," he summarized. "You see her go in the house?"

"No, not exactly. I saw her drive to the back of the house, and I know there's a back way in. I guess I assumed she went into the house. But I know she did, because she found Art. Anyway, I sat there in my car, stewing. God, I was upset. I wanted to storm in there and confront them, but what could I say? I wasn't really paying a lot of attention to the house, but when the other man came out, it caught my eye."

Straight's eyes narrowed. "What other man?" he asked mildly.

"The man with you," Rope explained. "He came out the front door and walked down to the car. I remember now the car was empty when I arrived."

Straight stared at Rope thoughtfully. Rope shifted his position uncomfortably. "What is it?" he asked nervously. "You knew I saw both of you, didn't you?"

"Sure," Straight said in a relaxed tone. "I'm trying to work out the time sequence, that's all. What did you see next?"

"You," Rope said. He began a detailed examination of his thumbnail. "You came out of the front door, too, carrying a bundle of some sort. You got in the car, and the other man drove off. I admit I was puzzled. I was beginning to think maybe the stories about Tracy and Art weren't true, after all. I stayed for about fifteen more minutes, then I heard a siren. It kept getting closer and closer and I guess I panicked. Anyway, I started the car and got the hell out of there. I never saw Tracy come out. I'd told the people at the store I was going to play golf," Rope concluded. "I had my clubs in the car, so I drove on out to the course and shot a round. I heard about Art in the clubhouse."

"News travels fast," Straight commented.

"It really does in this town," Rope said, as if afraid of being doubted. "God, I didn't know what to do."

"You still haven't explained why you didn't go to the law," Straight said.

"But I couldn't, don't you see? I would have had to explain what I was doing there, parked in front of Art's house. If Tracy found out I was following her, she'd never forgive me. She's a headstrong woman, and she's a great believer in freedom. She'd kick me aside like one of her out-of-date greeting cards if she knew I'd been snooping into her private life. Besides that, I was afraid the police might think I had done it."

"Why suspect you?" Straight asked.

"Well, Art and I were battling about whether or not he should sell our building. It was public knowledge I wanted him to sell and he refused to do it. And we had partner's insurance, so I actually made a tidy profit out of his death. There were just too many things like that. But I won't lie to you. The deciding factor was Tracy. With Art gone, I figured I could move in. And she means more to me than finding or punishing Art's killer does. Art had a lot of ways I didn't approve of. I can't say I'm too sorry to see him dead."

Rope looked at Straight hopefully. His eyes were pleading for the story to be believed. Straight returned Rope's gaze impassively. Again he allowed the silence to become protracted. Drops of perspiration beaded on Rope's forehead. The flecks in Straight's eyes seemed to move around as he watched Rope.

Finally Straight broke the silence. "Mr. Rope, that would be a hard story to dream up. I don't find it too difficult to accept. But I'm not convinced my employers would be willing to risk their freedom on your continued silence. You understand that, don't you?"

Rope tried to nod, and his head jerked convulsively.

Straight reached inside his jacket and revealed the .45 Colt.

Rope went pale again. Straight thought it was like watching the tide. He hefted the pistol but did not point it at Rope. Suddenly he realized he was whistling Tchaikovsky. He ceased and let silence fill the room once again.

Rope was mesmerized by the sudden appearance of the weapon. He couldn't have spoken even if he had anything to say. All he could do was wait.

Straight let him wait. The silence reached out, seemingly stretching to infinity. Straight let the gun rest on his leg. Rope's eyes followed the pistol.

Abruptly, Straight shoved the .45 back in its holster. The gun felt enormous to him, and he could imagine how it must look to Rope.

"I trust you, Mr. Rope," Straight said. "And, as I said, I place a high value on trust. It would distress me to discover you had betrayed my trust. Now, I'm not trying to terrorize you. I simply want to be positive you understand the consequences of any action you might take."

"All I want is to be left alone," Rope said hurriedly. "Hell, I told you the position I'm in. If I went to the law at this late date, they'd be all over me. Besides, everyone thinks it's a suicide. I'm not about to try to change anyone's mind."

"That's a wise policy, Mr. Rope," Straight told him. "Another thing you should understand: no police force will be able to protect you. If it should happen that the police latch on to you some way, don't believe what they tell you about protection. You've committed no crime unless they find out about you covering us up, so they won't have any levers to force you to talk. But it's possible someone besides us saw your car at Taber's. If they ask you about it, play dumb. And remember, you won't be able to hide from us. Certainly not in Oklahoma. There's not a police force in the state we can't penetrate. So you just keep on playing it cozy."

"I will," Rope said fervently. "I want to live. I don't want to cause you any trouble. And you don't have to worry about the police. I wouldn't tell them anything, anyway, but all we've got in Solano is a town marshal, and he does well to find his way to work in the mornings."

Straight nodded. "One more thing, Mr. Rope," he said, and swiveled his gaze to the bedroom.

Rope turned his head to see what the attraction was. Coady walked through the door. He seemed monstrous. He almost had to turn sideways to fit through the door. Coady grinned equally at Straight and Rope. He cracked his knuckles one at a time.

Rope started violently when he saw Coady. His eyes raced back and forth between Coady and Straight.

"You see how it is, Mr. Rope," Straight said calmly. "We can have you whenever we want you. And we'll know what you're doing. So don't get any foolhardy ideas."

"I swear . . ." Rope stammered.

Straight jerked his head at Coady. "Let's go," he said. "We can trust Mr. Rope."

Coady emitted his throaty laugh and followed Straight out of the apartment. He closed the door quietly after him.

Rope collapsed into the easy chair. His muscles were twitching. Involuntary tears rolled over his cheeks. "Oh, sweet Jesus," he murmured.

He went into the kitchen, poured a healthy slug of Scotch into a tumbler and choked it down straight. The whiskey quickly warmed him. His muscles stopped jerking. He refilled the tumbler and returned to the living room. Settling into the easy chair, he tried to think.

Things were closing in, no doubt about it. First Tracy hired some dick to snoop around, and now his life was being threatened. Rope couldn't see his way out. A competent detective would find out that he had been at Taber's house when the killing occurred. And his failure to mention it sure as hell made him look guilty. Who would believe his story—even if he could bring himself to tell it?

Rope set fire to a cigarette and cautiously peered out the window. The little man and his giant companion were evidently gone.

What to do?

Rope decided quickly. Despite the ominous little man's warning, he had faith in the law. Maybe not in Jamie Darden, but in the law in general. If he told them there was a murder and he had been threatened, they could protect him. It shouldn't take too long to capture the two men.

But not Jamie Darden.

Maneri watched his landlady pull into her driveway, then he drove out to the house she had rented him.

It wasn't much. A one-bedroom assembly with hardwood floors whose sheen was interrupted by furnace grates. The furniture matched the house in shabbiness.

Maneri used a glass of milk to wash down a stomach pill. The pill was a light blue-green and was stopping the secretion of saliva, along with other things. Maneri's mouth had been quite dry since he began taking the medicine and he resorted to beer to relieve the dryness.

The house was quiet. Maneri had had no opportunity to import his stereo, and the silence of the house oppressed him. He liked a little noise.

After leaving his new home, he guided Jerry Blefary's pickup to the Solano Inn. He parked by the entrance to the club and sauntered back to unit six.

Cranmer opened the door and tried to rub the sleep out of his eyes.

"You dogging it again in the afternoon?" Maneri asked.

Cranmer ignored him and went to the bathroom for some pills. Maneri turned on the radio in the room and the Osmond Brothers squeaked across the air. Cranmer emerged from the bathroom and switched off the radio. "Sounds like a torture rite," he muttered. "What's the scam on the widow?"

"That's one discreet lady," Maneri told him. "Tricky as a magician. She's got the whole town convinced she's shacked up in the City, right? Well, she's messing up some sheets all right, but not in Oklahoma City. How does Norman sound to you?"

"Terrific," Cranmer said. He rubbed his right knee.

"How does Kilduff in Norman sound to you?"

"Even better. The architect, huh?"

"Yeah," Maneri said. "The plot thins. I guess an architect could truly appreciate the design of the Taber broad's boobs."

Cranmer scratched his nose as the pills began to affect his nervous system. He lit a Camel and blew smoke at Maneri. "I'm beginning to see why Zantell doesn't buy the suicide story," he said. "Everywhere we look we find somebody with a solid reason for wanting Taber dead."

"Man was almost as popular as Nixon," said Maneri.

"Did Denise Taber go anywhere besides Kilduff's?"

"Nope. Straight up and straight back. They're pretty canny, though. Kilduff had a load of packages for her to bring home. I couldn't make out the labels, but I'm sure they came from Oklahoma City stores. Evidently he stocks up earlier in the week so she'll have material to prove she was in the City."

Cranmer nodded absently. "Wish Cindy would hustle up that financial report on Kilduff," he said. "Could be he and the widow worked it together. I can't picture him killing a man for a twelve-thousand-dollar commission, but a healthy inheritance would provide an extra incentive."

"Yeah, I suppose," said Maneri. "What did you come up with?"

"Mostly questions. I went through the Taber house, no problems. Think I picked up a couple of leads. For one, your beloved aunt may not be quite what she seems."

"Don't tell me you found the picture with the whips."

"Better than that. I nosed into a pile of canceled checks. Taber evidently wasn't too tidy. They were still in the bundles from the bank. I sorted through the latest bundle and found a check Taber had written to Tracy Zantell. One thousand dollars."

"These old cats like you have to buy their pussy," Maneri said.

"I'm shocked at your low opinion of your aunt. I didn't have time to run a complete audit, but I checked back six months. Six months, six checks, six thousand dollars. That's a lot to cough up just to get your end in."

"So he set her up," Maneri said. "I don't see where that's too surprising. She told us they were sharing a blanket. Stands to reason a cat with cash would spread it around."

"Well, I'll ask her about it. If she's as frank about this as she has been about everything else, she ought to clear the air quick enough."

"That all you found in the house?"

Cranmer shook his head. "What interests me most is something I didn't find."

"That's sensible," said Maneri.

"There's a desk in the study. That's where I found the checks. Desk has four drawers. One of them was locked. I unlocked it, and the damn thing was empty. Now, explain that. Why would somebody go to all the trouble of locking an empty drawer?"

"Give me a hint," Maneri requested.

"It doesn't lock automatically," Cranmer continued. "I had to pick it shut. And the drawer doesn't have any false sides or bottom or anything like that."

"How's this?" Maneri said. "Normally there's something kept locked up. Say Taber kept his razor there. And say Taber has faith in locks. So when he checks on the razor, he doesn't go to the bother of opening the drawer and actually looking at it. He just makes sure the drawer is still locked. Now, say the wife wants the razor. She knows Taber's habits. So she filches the blade and relocks the drawer. Taber doesn't know it's gone because he just tugs at the drawer once in a while. But when supersleuth ransacks the house he finds the empty drawer. Like it?"

"It scans," said Cranmer. "But why doesn't she put it back after Taber croaks?"

"Incriminating," said Maneri.

"Then why doesn't she unlock the drawer?"

"She's too busy fucking the architect. It slips her mind."

"But if it's worth all the subterfuge . . ."

"Remember," Maneri interrupted, "she's not expecting anyone to pry into the desk. From what I hear about the local law, they might not even be able to get in with a key."

"That's right enough," Cranmer agreed. "I think that marshal has been thrown off too many rodeos."

"I'm going to have to take you to a rodeo one of these days," Maneri said. "Your vision seems to lack authenticity."

Cranmer lit another Camel, leaned back on the bed and blew smoke at the ceiling. The smoke curled through the air and nearly asphyxiated an innocent spider.

"I also got to know that goddamned cat," Cranmer said. "I wanted to watch him open the bathroom door, so I locked myself in there with him. Goddamn cat curled up and went to sleep. I even stretched out on the floor and pretended I was dead. He still wouldn't open the door."

Maneri broke up. "Pretended you were dead? Fantastic. I always knew you could teach me the tricks of the trade. How do you pretend you're dead?"

Cranmer scowled at him. "I lay down in about the position Taber was in and tried not to breathe too damn loud."

"So what happened?"

"Goddamn cat came over and licked me on the face."

Maneri clapped his hands and cackled. "How long did you stay on the floor, dad?"

"Damn near a half-hour," Cranmer said sourly. "I told you I was going to need a good supply of booze to make it through this farce. Cats that open doors. Jesus Christ."

"Maybe you discovered an important character trait of the cat's," Maneri said, only half kidding. "If you could prove he won't open the door when he's got company, you'd blow the marshal's suicide theory out the chimney."

"The thought occurred to me," Cranmer said sardonically. "Want a drink?"

"Yeah, all right. Medicine man said to drink liquor."

Cranmer splashed bourbon into a couple of glasses and handed one to Maneri. Maneri used the bourbon to wash down a pill.

"Stomach medicine?" asked Cranmer.

"Dexamyl," said Maneri. "I'm not as young as I used to be. I can't handle these sleepless nights."

"Why not go home and go to bed?"

"I've got a date with Miss Henning tonight. She's going to demonstrate her culinary skills."

"I bet she is," Cranmer said. "You better keep an eye out for the boy friend."

"He doesn't worry me," said Maneri. "He's a clown. I really ought to thank him for picking the fight. Word spreads fast in these small towns. I'll be a folk hero by midnight."

Maneri grinned and Cranmer shook his head.

"You get your bets down?" Maneri asked.

"Yep. I put five hundred dollars on each team."

"Texas, Air Force and Tennessee?"

"Correct."

"Whoopee! Last of the riverboat gamblers. Say, I found a poker game for you if you're in the market."

"I might be," Cranmer said. "There's no ball game tomorrow night. Where's the game?"

"Well, it shifts around. What you do is call Information. The operator knows where they are."

"You're not serious," Cranmer protested. "The telephone operator?"

"Why not?"

Cranmer shrugged. "I'll bear it in mind. Oh, I went out to the golf course and checked up Rope. He played all right. But he didn't show up until about one. So he was loose during the time that counts. His caddy said he shot a miserable round. He's normally an eight handicap, the fellow said, but he shot in the nineties last Thursday."

"Did he have bloodstained hands?" Maneri joked.

"Nobody mentioned it. I tell you, I like this Rope more and more all the time. We've got his car at Taber's at lunchtime; he's Taber's partner, so he probably made a profit from his death; we've got him chasing Taber's woman; and we've got him upset and shooting a lousy round of golf right after the kill."

"There's quite a few assumptions tied up in there," Maneri complained. "But here's another thing. I think I've figured what the little girl meant about Rope having an eagle on his forehead."

"What's that?"

"Well, he went to play golf, right? Golfers wear caps. And an eagle is some kind of hot shit in golf. So why not have Rope wearing a golf cap with an eagle on the front?"

Cranmer nodded. "I've seen caps like that. It's a good chance. Listen, Butch, I've got two things I want you to look into. First, find out about the partnership arrangement. Were Taber and Rope reciprocating beneficiaries on any insurance policies? What's Rope planning to do with his half of the store? Sell it for a courthouse? Et cetera. Then I want you to run up to Ponca City Saturday. See what you can find out about the Tabers' activities when they lived there. That's kind of a short straw, but it needs doing if we're going to charge Zantell enough to pay our expenses."

Maneri said, "Ponca City. That's where Taber used to operate his jewelry racket?"

"So Zantell says. It'll give you a chance to limber up the Fiat."

Maneri sighed. "I'm afraid to ask what you'll be doing," he said.

"Why, hell," said Cranmer, "I have to watch the ball game to see how my bet comes out."

"Yeah," Maneri said resignedly. "Say, I thought of something you overlooked."

"Not surprising."

"You said Kilduff and Denise Taber might have been in this together. But didn't you tell me Kilduff was at some Rotary Club or other last Thursday?"

"Kiwanis," said Cranmer.

"Whatever. And you verified it?"

"Correct."

Maneri spread his hands.

The telephone buzzed before Cranmer could figure out a way to get Kilduff from the Kiwanis luncheon in Norman to the Taber house. He hoisted himself off the bed and limped across the room to the phone.

An unfamiliar voice said, "Is this Steve Cranmer?"

"That's who," Cranmer said. "Who's this?"

"My name is Michael Rope . . ."

"Yeah, I know who you are," Cranmer interrupted.

"Good. That'll save time. Listen, I have some information

about Art Taber that should interest you. I don't want to go into detail over the phone, but I can tell you he didn't commit suicide. He was killed, murdered, and I know who did it."

"Yeah? Who?"

"I don't have a name. But I can give you perfect descriptions of them. But listen, they threatened to kill me if I told. I need protection."

There was a pause. Then Cranmer said, "You said 'them' and 'they,' Mr. Rope. Are you saying there's more than one killer?"

"Two. They threatened me with a gun. They said they would know what I'm doing, but I'm sure that's a bluff. There's no way they could know who I telephone."

"Unless they've got the phone tapped," Cranmer said cheerily. "I don't suppose that's too likely. Why don't you come on over and tell me about it, Mr. Rope? I assume you've checked me out with Tracy Zantell."

"She told me about you," Rope said. "That's how I knew where to call. I don't trust our police to be able to help me."

"Well, I don't swear I can help you, Mr. Rope, but I won't wave a gun at you. I'm in room six at this dump."

"Couldn't you come over here? I'm afraid they might be waiting outside."

There was another pause. Then Cranmer totally confused Rope by asking, "Do you have a color television?"

Rope muttered, "Yes."

"All right, I'll drift by. You can give me the story and the descriptions, and then we can watch the World Series. Does that sound all right to you?"

"I guess that's all right, Mr. Cranmer," he said. "But I really can't imagine sitting around and watching a ball game with a couple of murderers stalking around outside."

"There won't be anything for us to do tonight, anyway," Cranmer assured him. "Where are you?"

After Rope gave Cranmer the directions to the Floodtide Apartments, he cradled the receiver, then remained by the phone, staring at his door and trying to figure out what was going on. He came to the conclusion Tracy had hired a maniac.

Finally he got up, crossed the room and poured another slug

of Scotch into his glass. Downing half of it in a single swallow, he refilled the glass, dropped in a couple of ice cubes and returned to his living room. The sound of the wind made him twitch. He glanced around the apartment fearfully and wished Cranmer would hurry.

Rope had a cigarette in his mouth and was reaching for the lighter on his coffee table when he heard the sound of the wind again, and the door to his apartment swung open.

Straight and Coady traversed the obstacle course of the littered vacant lot.

"I think we threw a pretty solid scare into him," said Straight. "I actually empathize with the man. Try to put yourself inside his skin, Ham. This may be a typical day for you and me, but that man's not accustomed to violence, threats and death. Probably his parents died and that's as close as he's ever been before. And now we've removed all his options. I may compose a philosophical treatise," he continued. "Concerning the effect of the abrupt intrusion of a foreign element on the life of an ordinary man. I think most of us drift through life in our preconceived ruts without ever becoming aware of the sameness of our days. But all it takes is one totally foreign situation to rekindle our minds, force us out of our ruts. The interesting thing is we always settle into a new rut."

Coady had obviously quit listening.

"How do you calculate Rope's reaction?" Straight asked.

Coady shrugged.

"Weren't you listening?"

"Nah, I skimmed over most of it."

They climbed into the rented Impala. Coady reached for the ignition, then patted his pockets. "Shit," he said. "I must've left the keys in the apartment. Back in a minute."

Straight shook his head. He would have to give McEachern a negative report on his man from the West Coast.

Straight settled back in the car seat and considered the intrusion of alien activities and emotions. In a few minutes Coady came trotting across the vacant lot. He leaped in the car and shoved the key into the ignition.

"I had to waste him, Spinoza," he said matter-of-factly.

"What! Goddamnit, why did you have . . .?"

"He was calling law when I got back up there," Coady explained defensively. "Some guy named Cranmer. The guy was on his way over. Rope was going to spill his guts. I heard him talking on the telephone."

Straight rapped his knuckles against the windshield. "I told them to leave well enough alone," he said. "This Cranmer, did you hang a first name on him?"

"Nah. Just Mr. Cranmer. Must be local law, huh?"

Straight shook his head. "Local man's named Darden," he said. "I worked with a fellow named Steve Cranmer once. He was with the government. Not too clever, but mean as hell. If he's still with the government, and if he's the same guy, and if he's working on this case, Taber might be a lot more important than we gave him credit for."

"So what do we do?" asked Coady.

"Bury ourselves in Medwick and wait," Straight said. "Man, this is going to blow the hell out of the notion Taber killed himself. Did you hang around the apartment long enough to wipe prints?"

"Sure," Coady said. "I know how to handle that stuff."

Somehow Straight doubted that.

Once again Maneri borrowed Jerry Blefary's pickup. He dropped Cranmer off at the Floodtide Apartments. They had decided Maneri should stay clear of the meeting so he could maintain his cover.

Cranmer limped up the stairs and knocked on Rope's door. The impact of his hand caused the door to swing in. Cranmer pushed the door open the rest of the way with his cane. Rope's body was visible from the doorway.

Cranmer's expression didn't alter. He stood for a full minute, listening. No sound came from within the apartment. Cranmer limped over to the body, felt for a pulse, found none, and stared curiously at Rope's mangled windpipe. Maybe the phone *was* tapped, he thought.

He searched the apartment quickly and efficiently. He found a golf cap bearing an eagle, but nothing else of interest. After a brief mental debate Cranmer telephoned the Solano marshal.

Five

Jamie Darden drew the six of diamonds. He slipped the card between the seven and five of diamonds and triumphantly discarded the ace of clubs, face down.

"Gin," he said.

Sheriff Burwell Santo toted up the points remaining in his hand. Darden computed his new total painstakingly, gathered the cards and began shuffling awkwardly.

Santo was concerned. He owned a small ranch south of Solano which depended on LP gas for heating. As yet, he had been unable to acquire his supply for the winter. Santo believed the energy shortage was apocryphal, the result of a conspiracy among huge corporations which weren't satisfied with a man's right arm but wanted the left as well.

The telephone in Darden's small office interrupted his tirade. Darden laboriously completed the deal, then picked up the phone. His aim was a little shaky and he knocked the cowboy hat off his head with the receiver. Cursing, he finally located his ear. "Marshal's office, Darden," he grumbled. "Yeah . . . No shit? . . . Yeah, I know where he lives. Don't touch nothing. We'll be out in a minute."

Darden replaced the receiver and stared at Santo glumly. "You ready for this?" he asked. "We got another body."

Santo cocked his eyebrows. "Whose?"

"Mike Rope. That insurance investigator from the City found him dead in his apartment."

"What happened?"

"Christ knows. Cranmer called it a murder."

Santo rubbed his chin thoughtfully. "Rope lives out at the Floodtide, don't he?"

"Yeah."

"Well, looks like you've got another one to go with Taber."

"No way," Darden protested. "The Floodtide's outside the city limits. That makes it your case, Burwell."

The two lawmen walked out to Darden's car.

"You're wrong, Jamie," said Santo. "Remember, they extended the city limits after they built those apartments. It's in your jurisdiction now."

Darden started the engine and hit the siren. He roared down Solano's abbreviated Main Street with the siren wailing, made a U turn at the Solano Inn, then screeched back through the business section. Both Darden and Santo sat in their seats importantly.

As they neared the Floodtide Apartments, Darden slowed the car and searched for the sign which marked Solano's city limits. "Goddamn," he said. The sign was no longer where he thought it should be.

He drove on past the building, siren screaming. Two hundred yards beyond was the city limit sign. Darden made another tire-eating U turn and returned to the Floodtide Apartments.

Santo was chuckling. "A murder a week makes Solano unique," he said. "But don't worry about it, Jamie. Maybe you can find a good job as a coach."

"What do you mean, 'a murder a week'?" Darden muttered. "It's not my fault Taber killed himself. And this here ain't necessarily a murder, either."

"Keep telling yourself that," Santo instructed.

They climbed the stairs to Rope's apartment. The door was ajar, so they went on in. Rope's body was on the floor by the living-room wall. Cranmer sat in a chair a few feet from the corpse. He was watching the ball game on television.

Darden and Santo gaped at him. Cranmer watched Jerry Koosman deliver a strike, then glanced over at the lawmen and said, "Gentlemen."

"Hello, Cranmer," said Darden. He looked at the body nervously. "What's the story?"

"No score yet," Cranmer said. "But they've just begun." He grinned and lit a cigarette.

Santo and Darden traded disbelieving glances.

"Rope called me," Cranmer said, his eyes still on the television screen. "Said he had something important to tell me, something that would prove Taber was murdered. But he wouldn't talk about it on the phone. So I came over here and found him like this."

Darden looked down at the body. "Strangled, huh?" he said.

"Looks like," Cranmer said.

Darden continued to stare at the body as if immobilized.

Koosman retired the Athletics, and Cranmer looked at Darden curiously as a commercial erupted. "You got a coroner in this town?" he asked.

Darden pulled his eyes away from Rope. "Dr. Keating is kind of a medical examiner, I guess," he said.

"So why not get him out here?"

Darden nodded. Santo sat on the couch. It wasn't his case, so he could enjoy watching Darden fumble.

Darden walked to the phone, reached for it, hesitated, then pulled a dirty handkerchief from his pocket. He used the handkerchief to keep his hand from touching the receiver.

Cranmer shook his head and returned to the ball game.

It took nearly two hours to complete Solano's version of a police investigation. Cranmer watched the ball game—on a color TV—and drank Rope's Scotch.

Dr. Keating showed up with an ambulance, and after Darden outlined the position of the body and took a few Polaroid photographs, Rope's remains were removed. Keating left with them.

Darden was irritated. He'd had a hell of a time marking the position of the body. His chalk refused to write on the shag carpet. But with the body out of the room, the marshal relaxed enough to begin questioning Cranmer.

The Mets were leading 2–0. After Tug McGraw pitched his way out of a bases-loaded jam, Cranmer let Darden turn off the television.

Cranmer recited the details of his phone call from Rope three times. He said only that Rope had told him two men were involved and they had threatened him. He said nothing about the black Lincoln which had been parked by Taber's house. He said nothing about Maneri or Tracy Zantell.

After asking the few questions he could think of, Darden let Cranmer go.

Cranmer picked up the telephone without benefit of a handkerchief and called a cab. Ten minutes later he was back at the Solano Inn. Cranmer was moving in a gentle fog. He had used Rope's Scotch to wash down a pair of Demerols, and the drug had conquered his system.

Cranmer limped unsteadily to room six. The knob turned in his hand and he walked into the room, wondering why he could never remember to lock doors. He had the vague impression someone else was in the room. Before his fuzzy brain could signal his body of danger, something smashed into the back of his head.

The Demerol numbed the pain, but the blackness was still a relief.

Maneri choked down a glass of milk before dinner, then drank wine with the spaghetti Martha Henning had prepared. The meal was nothing to write songs about.

A jazz concert followed dinner. Martha had an excellent collection of elderly jazz records. Early Ellington, even some Jelly Roll Morton.

Maneri smoked a joint occasionally to maintain his high. Martha refused to join him, but she continued to drink wine.

When Artie Shaw's *Concerto for Clarinet* dropped onto the turntable, Martha moved to sit beside Maneri on the couch. He kissed her leisurely, expecting nothing, and was pleasantly surprised when her mouth opened. Her tongue explored his. Soon their hands were busy.

Maneri led her into the bedroom. Her body still looked like a model's. But she put moves on him like a stripper.

Cranmer's mind climbed out of the proverbial well. It was not a new experience for him. The pain in his head and the flashing lights in his eyes didn't frighten him. He realized instantly he had suffered no damage, and the memory of what had happened was clear.

He kept his eyes shut and let his ears do the work. He assumed he was still in the motel room. He was lying on a thinly carpeted floor, which fit the motel theory. And he could hear another person breathing in the room.

Cranmer allowed his right eye to flicker open and shut. He was in the motel room. A man was sitting in the room's one chair, evidently waiting for Cranmer to awaken. There was no gun visible in Cranmer's brief glance. He shifted his left arm a bit and realized there was also no gun in his shoulder holster.

The situation was bad enough. Cranmer's leg prevented him from leaping into action, and it also lessened his chances of coming out on top in a hand-to-hand battle. Without moving or opening his eyes, he said quietly, "I guess I must have the wrong room."

The man in the chair gave a quick imitation of a kangaroo. Cranmer rolled up to a sitting position and examined his assailant. He had never seen him before. The man wore a cheap brown suit and a rumpled tie. He had enough size for a football player. His eyes were round and unintelligent.

"Mind if I stand up?" Cranmer asked mildly.

The man made an upward motion with his hand.

Cranmer found his cane and used it to lever himself off the floor. He limped to the dresser, poured a shot of bourbon and swallowed a couple of pills. Then he sat on the bed. "Did I interrupt something?" he said.

The man in the brown suit handed him a business card wordlessly. Cranmer read it impassively. It told him that Arnold Dreiser was a claims investigator for the company which had insured Arthur Taber.

"Light dawns," Cranmer murmured.

"Understand you've been inpersonating me," said Dreiser. He towered over Cranmer.

Cranmer looked up at him and said, "How could I impersonate you, friend? I've never heard of you."

"You've been hanging around Denise Taber."

"True."

"You told her you were with our company."

"True."

"So what's the real story?"

Cranmer finished his bourbon, sighed and handed Dreiser his detective license. Dreiser read it slowly.

"I'm investigating Arthur Taber's death," Cranmer said. "My client doesn't want to be identified, so I said I was investigating for the insurance company. Why get mad at me just because you didn't have the sense to be suspicious?"

"Taber committed suicide," Dreiser stated firmly.

Cranmer gave what he hoped was a mysterious laugh.

"You come up with something?" asked Dreiser.

"If I had, I wouldn't tell you," Cranmer said. "I may prefer assault charges."

"Shit. Quit rubbing our name in the dirt, Cranmer. I only gave you a sample, a warning. I'm willing to convince you some more if you demand it."

"Oh, that's all right," Cranmer said. "You take my gun?"

Dreiser nodded. "I stuck it under your pillow."

"Did you folks have any insurance on Taber's partner, Michael Rope?"

"That's our business."

"Yeah. Well, in case you're interested, he died tonight."

Dreiser's eyes widened. "How?"

"That's my business." Cranmer laughed.

Dreiser took a step forward. "Now look, Jackson, don't get snotty with me or I'll lay you out again. It ain't much of a challenge, but you make me enjoy my work."

Cranmer grinned at him. The one step had brought the insurance man within range of Cranmer's cane. Keeping the friendly smile on his face, Cranmer struck with the cane.

It was a perfect shot to the crotch. The impact made a dull splat in the room. Dreiser doubled over. Using his left leg as an anchor, Cranmer rose from the bed swinging his right fist. At the peak of its momentum, the fist smashed into Dreiser's face. He fell backward like a dead man.

The force of the blow knocked Cranmer back onto the bed. He stood up slowly, using his cane, and looked at the insurance man dispassionately. Then he broke his nose with the cane.

When Dreiser woke up, Cranmer was sitting in the room's single chair sipping bourbon. His pistol was leveled at Dreiser.

"Go away," Cranmer told him. "All you had to do was ask, but you had to get rough, didn't you? Well, that's just a sample, a warning. Stay away from me."

Dreiser couldn't decide whether to hold his crotch or his nose. He left the room without speaking.

Cranmer chuckled and ate some Demerol.

Cranmer strode briskly through an enormous building, perhaps a part of a military base. He was wearing only a pair of boxer shorts. His skin was almost black from the sun.

He was tracking a sound, but he didn't know what was making it or why it was significant. He knew he had to find the source. It might have been a human voice, but he only heard the sound intermittently. Yet it was an important sound. Each time it drifted through the air of the enormous building, one of Cranmer's friends would come up to him and shake his hand and distract his attention just long enough for the sound to fade.

It was wonderful to know so many people and have so many close friends, but their timing disturbed Cranmer.

Two women approached Cranmer. As they neared, he saw they were clad only in panties. Four breasts loomed large and vibrant. The nipples were hungry red eyes. Once again the air vibrated with the sound. This time Cranmer could tell it was coming from his left, and he spun away from the four breasts and began running down a wide corridor. He still couldn't identify the sound, though.

Cranmer saw a flight of stairs going down. It seemed odd to him there were no stairs reaching up, but he knew he did not have the time to consider it. He leaped down the stairs three at a time. Although he was concerned about the sound, he exulted in racing down the stairs. The impact of hitting each stair made his knees flex, and the muscles in his legs rippled darkly. Then he was running down sand stairs. The sand surrounded his feet, impeding his progress. He had to pull each foot free before he could take the next three-stair leap. His feet made no sound in the sand, and he remembered his feet had made no sound on the wooden stairs he had been descending previously.

He heard the important sound again, and he was in a ballroom. A band was playing "Mood Indigo." The band was adequate, but one of the clarinets was half a step flat. This gave the song even more of a minor, melancholy cast. But the flat clarinet was not the sound Cranmer had been tracking.

Maneri was in the ballroom, huddled against the wall. Cranmer, dressed now in a white suit, tried to traverse the room to reach Maneri. But his friends kept stopping him. There were many people he hadn't seen for years, and they all recognized him and smiled when they saw him. The two women appeared again, wearing evening gowns, and Cranmer led them over to Maneri. He wanted to comfort the friendless man. Each woman held onto one of Cranmer's arms. He could feel their breasts burning holes in his white suit. Maneri watched them shyly.

Blood was meant for bleeding, said Maneri.

Cranmer watched Maneri's nose shatter, and he watched the blood spread over Maneri's face.

The band continued giving "Mood Indigo" a melancholy cast, and Cranmer cast a fly into a red stream. An important sound was coming from beneath the water, and he was hoping to capture the sound with the fly. The water was warm and flowed gently over Cranmer's body in the red swimsuit. Cranmer began swimming across the stream in a powerful crawl. His legs beat the water, and he exulted in his strength.

Cranmer swam through a trapdoor and was once again in the enormous building. Now he believed he was in the Sacramento Air Matériel Area, SMAMA. He could no longer hear the sound, and a deep sadness engulfed him. The building was empty now, and Cranmer had to fight back the tears.

He was face down in the sand. The sand was malevolent, alive. It covered his arms and then crawled over his legs. He felt the bullet enter his right knee and knew he would never be able to pull himself out of the sand. All of his body was under the sand now except his face. And the sand was grasping for his nose. He knew if the sand captured his nose he would die. For a moment he welcomed the thought. But then he heard the important sound again, and he began to struggle. He heaved himself up, but he could not escape the sand. He heaved once more.

Cranmer woke up and gasped for breath. There was no feeling in his arms, which had been pillowing his head.

He struggled loose from the covers and sat on the edge of the bed. "Jesus Christ," he said aloud.

He massaged his arms until they tingled. His breathing evened. The motel room was overheated and glowed from the outside lights. Cranmer lit a cigarette and coughed. The fear was still strong in him. The burning tobacco made an important sound in the room.

Cranmer turned on the light beside the bed, walked into the bathroom and drank some water.

One of these days I'm going to take enough of an overdose to keep me under, he thought. It had happened before. Each time he had managed to wake up. What worried him was the notion the sand might one day bury him.

His nerves were still quivering, so he began to read a paperback book called *Mouthful.* He read for two hours and wondered why he never met a woman like that. Then he could go back to sleep.

Richard Straight took a sip from his cup of boiled water and looked doubtfully at Ham Coady. Coady was watching a television soap opera and drinking beer. Straight waited until the music faded dramatically into a commercial, then said, "There's something I'm curious about, Ham."

"About what, Spinoza?"

"Rope said he saw you going into the Taber house. Said you only stayed for a minute, then came back out again. You never said anything about going into the house."

Coady hesitated a moment, watching the TV screen. He said "When?" unconvincingly.

Straight just looked at him.

Coady downed his beer and crumpled the can. "Oh, I know what he's talking about," he said. "When I saw that car parked down the street, I went in to warn you. After I saw he was just going to sit there. But as soon as I get inside the house, this woman comes wandering in from the back. So I duck back out again, quick."

Straight took a swallow of boiled water. Like a modern poem, the story didn't scan. He couldn't imagine Coady letting the woman go upstairs unhampered. It was something to keep in mind, but he didn't pursue it.

"I think the time has come for us to do a little work on our own," he told Coady.

"Such as?"

"Such as keeping track of what's going on in Solano. It seems evident our bosses are willing to let us drift out here. But I don't like drifting. Especially if Cranmer is who I think he is. He'll be moving in on us, and he's the type of character who'd shoot you four times while you were cracking your knuckles. Look, the most logical course for us to follow is to go home, right? They'd have a hell of a time finding us if we weren't hanging around waiting for them. But do you want to leave without instructions?"

Coady gave his rumbling laugh. "I'm not too crazy about taking a shit without orders," he said.

"Correct. So we have no option. But we can choose between sitting in this room waiting for disaster and getting into the stream of things to keep tabs on the progress of the investigation. I vote for locating Cranmer and trailing him."

Coady shrugged. "That's fine with me. My butt's tired of sitting here watching you drink water."

Straight's chilly smile made Coady's eyes shift back to the television.

Cranmer rapped on Tracy Zantell's door with his cane at 12:20 Friday. He'd called earlier, and she said she was keeping the gift shop closed because of Rope's death.

Tracy answered the door. She was still wearing a robe, but her face and hair had been organized for the day. Cranmer wangled a glass of bourbon, and they sat in the living room.

"Well now," Cranmer said, "it seems like your boyfriends have a high mortality rate."

"I'm the town's only unmarried widow," Tracy said bitterly. "What happened to Mike? All I've heard is the gossip around town."

Cranmer told her about the phone call and finding the body.

"But how would he know it was a murder?" Tracy protested. "Who would be threatening him?"

"The murderers would be threatening him," Cranmer said. "And he knew it was a murder because he was hanging around the Taber house when it happened."

He told her about the little girl and the black Lincoln. "We had Rope pegged for it till he called. Figured he was jealous and following you around. You ever notice him tailing you?"

Tracy shook her head. "It's possible, though," she said. "He had this outlandish notion of marrying me. And I don't go around peering over my shoulder."

"Maybe you should," Cranmer said. "How close were you and Rope before Taber died?"

"Not very. Dinner a couple of times, but nothing serious. No sex."

"And after Taber died?"

"Sex, but still nothing serious."

Cranmer made an indistinct sound and lit a Camel. "Why did Taber pay you a thousand dollars a month?" he asked abruptly.

Tracy's eyes widened a little. "My," she said, "you have been snooping around."

"You hired me to do it."

"Right. Well, it's kind of an interesting story at that. You see, I come from Ponca City too. And I had a little something on Art. Enough to put him away for a while, but mainly enough to spoil his reputation—and he was more concerned about that. To give it its proper name, I was blackmailing him. He bought the gift shop for me and gave me a thousand a month."

She watched Cranmer as if to gauge his reaction. He sipped bourbon impassively. "What did you have on him?" he asked.

Tracy shook her head emphatically. "Let the past die," she said. "It was nothing that would affect his murder."

Cranmer scowled but let it go. "Seems like an odd way to start a love affair," he commented.

"Oh, we had one beautiful scene. One day I went to his house to collect. He was seething. Started screaming about how he didn't have to pay me anything. Fortunately I was wearing a skimpy dress that day. He grabbed me and started shaking me. I don't think he really planned anything violent; he was hoping to scare me off. But I guess you know how any strong emotion can turn sexual. And I suppose if it hadn't been for the blackmail, we'd have gotten together even sooner—the attraction was there. Somehow he forgot why he was shaking me and got preoccupied with the various parts of me that were shaking. We ended up on the floor like a couple of high school kids. After that, he didn't mind paying the money."

"Terrific," Cranmer said. "Well, the main reason I came by was to see if you want us to keep on with the investigation. The law knows Taber was murdered now, and that's what you were after, isn't it?"

"I want you to continue," Tracy said. "Have you seen Jamie Darden operate?"

Cranmer grinned.

"That's what I mean," said Tracy. "I want the murderer caught and punished."

"I may have to drop my insurance cover and admit I'm working for you. I had a visit from the real insurance investigator last night."

"Say what you want. I don't care if people know you're working for me. The insurance thing was your idea anyway."

Cranmer nodded and finished his drink. "It might help if you told me what you had on Taber. It could fit in in a way you haven't considered."

Tracy shook her head again, and Cranmer sighed. "Rope said two people were involved," he said. "Can you think of any likely teams?"

"No."

"Yeah. Well, I'll be in touch."

Cranmer limped to the door. He wondered obscurely what would happen if he grabbed Tracy and started shaking her.

She'd probably kick my knee, he thought.

Cranmer dialed 411 and absently considered the brown Malibu which had been parked in front of the Solano Inn. The driver of the Malibu had had a white bandage covering his nose. Odds were it was Dreiser, the insurance investigator. But was he lying in wait or simply keeping tabs on Cranmer?

"Directory assistance," said the professionally cheerful operator's voice.

"Where's the poker game tonight?" Cranmer asked, feeling foolish.

But without hesitation the operator said, "Room 236 of the Gentry Hotel in Medwick."

"Medwick?"

"Yes, sir."

Cranmer replaced the phone glumly. Then he remembered he was on an expense account, so he phoned a cab. It would be an expensive journey, but the client could foot the bill.

The brown Malibu followed Cranmer's cab to Medwick. The glare of the headlights obscured the driver, but when the taxi let Cranmer out at the Gentry Hotel, he glanced back and spotted the white bandage.

Ignoring Dreiser, Cranmer paid the tab and rode the elevator to the second floor of the hotel. He knocked on the door to room 236. After a moment a man wearing a western shirt with snaps instead of buttons opened the door.

"Got room for another in the poker game?" Cranmer asked.

"Poker game?" The man raised incredulous eyebrows. "You must have the wrong room, mister."

"It's all right, Phil," said a voice from inside the room. "I know him."

Cranmer limped into the room as the man in the western shirt backed out of the way. Solano's mayor, Peter Brindle, said, "Hello, Mr. Cranmer. Didn't know you were a cardplayer."

"Just a dabbler," said Cranmer. "I hate to knock your town, but the pace is slow."

"So it is, for a fact," said Brindle. "Pull up a chair."

Cranmer joined the game. There were five other men sitting around a green-felt-covered table. The table had slots for poker chips and recessed cork-lined spaces for drinks. The game of the night seemed to be seven stud. Cranmer preferred five-card games, but he knew how to take advantage of the extra two cards.

Three hours later the other men were wishing Cranmer had been denied entrance. The game had a limit of only fifty dollars, but Cranmer was up nearly a thousand by playing his quiet, unspectacular game.

Brindle was the only man in the room whom Cranmer knew. And Brindle was losing heavily. He played an almost desperate, hopeful type of poker which was the equivalent of slow suicide.

Cranmer returned to the table after a trip to the bathroom for a Demerol dosage. Brindle was dealing. "This is going to be seven card, high low split," said the mayor.

Cranmer exchanged a weary glance with the man who had been guarding the door. This was the kind of game losers dealt. Brindle, wearing another pair of overalls, or perhaps the same pair Cranmer had seen him in the other day, flipped the cards around the table. Cranmer's first up card was the seven of spades.

Possible low hand, he thought as he picked up his two down cards. They were the four and five of spades. Possible straight flush and a solid low hand.

Brindle bet fifty, and all the other players called.

Cranmer's next card was the six of spades. Brindle had a pair of tens showing. Cranmer just called, testing the water. The man in the western shirt, Phil, raised twenty-five, and Brindle raised him back fifty. Cranmer continued to call, content to let the others build the pot. All the players stayed. Dreams of drawing the perfect three cards filled their minds.

Cranmer's next card was the ace of diamonds, giving him a seventy-six for low. The only other player to improve his hand on the board was Brindle, who dealt himself a third ten. Brindle and Phil continued to control the betting.

Brindle dealt Cranmer the jack of clubs. No help. Phil kept betting strong, raising Brindle, who raised him back until they reached the three raise limit. Phil had an eight, deuce, trey and four showing. He was obviously shooting for a low hand, and Brindle was playing high.

Brindle dealt the seventh card around the table, face down. Cranmer glanced at his card casually. It was the three of spades.

Brindle bet fifty. His three tens were still high on the board. This time Cranmer raised fifty. Phil looked at him skeptically. Cranmer's visible hand of ace, jack, seven and six wasn't overly impressive. But omitting the jack indicated a possible strong low, and Phil had been watching Cranmer collect chips all night, so he just called.

The other players dropped out, their dreams unfulfilled.

But Brindle was ecstatic. He was grinning and talking more than he had all night. He had an apparent lock, with both Cranmer and Phil going low. Brindle raised.

Cranmer raised him another fifty, the third raise.

Phil and Brindle called. Brindle immediately said, "Look at these sweethearts, by God. About time I got some luck." He turned over the fourth ten.

Phil shrugged. "Eighty-four for low," he said. "I couldn't fill the son of a bitch."

Cranmer moved the ace and jack aside and without speaking lined up the three, four, five, six and seven of spades.

Phil grinned resignedly. Brindle literally sagged in his chair. His face turned gray. "Excuse me," he said stiffly. He stood up and walked to the bathroom.

Cranmer raked in the pot, just under three thousand dollars.

"Now you done made the mayor sick," Phil said.

Cranmer grinned at him and started stacking his chips. "He usually lose this much?" he asked.

"Well, it's been a while since he had a really good night," Phil said noncommittally.

"Cash me in," said Cranmer. "I'm sure you folks don't mind if I quit while I'm ahead."

"Just wish I could ever get ahead so I could quit," said Phil cheerfully.

Cranmer's chips amounted to nearly four thousand dollars. Not bad for small-town poker, he thought. He would have to remember to thank Maneri for steering him to the game.

"Cranmer's in the hotel," Straight told Coady.

"Nah."

"I saw him in the lobby. He's hobbling around on a cane and his hair's a little gray around the edges now, but it's him all right. He went up to the second floor."

"So what's on the second floor?"

Straight shrugged. "He may be checking all the hotels. I

suggest we get the car and wait for him out front. If he knew we were here, I never would have seen him. So he must be groping. Let's drift along with him and see where he gropes."

They had switched the Impala for a Dodge Dart. They parked across the street from the Gentry Hotel and waited. It was a three-hour vigil. And Straight quickly spotted the brown Malibu.

"Could be a back-up man," he theorized.

But when Cranmer limped out of the hotel, he climbed into a cab. The brown Malibu trailed the cab to the Solano Inn. Straight and Coady drove discreetly behind the Malibu.

"Looks like someone else is interested in him," said Coady. "I remember I got into a deal like this once in Minneapolis. Had to take out the snoop before I could get to the target, and I damn near lost the target fooling around with the snoop."

"He must know the Malibu's following him," Straight said. "He also must not care. That gives us an interesting opportunity."

"Yeah? What's that?"

Straight explained it to him.

Cranmer dialed Maneri's number. It was well after midnight, but Maneri's "Hello" was alert and cheerful.

"You have a nice day with the road gang?" Cranmer asked.

"Truly exhilarating. There were a few comments made about my working only two and a half days out of four, but my native charm kept everyone friendly."

"Guess you know we lost our number-one suspect."

"Yeah, that's a shame."

"Have you got that broad with you?"

"Which one?"

"The jewelry clerk."

"Yeah, dad. She's sleeping at the moment. She's upset. She's running out of bosses. Say, I found out what Taber kept in that locked drawer. An address book."

"Terrific. A really significant piece of data. Why lock up an address book?"

"You're the sleuth, dad. I just furnish the raw material. Martha was over at the Taber house once when the old man needed a phone number. He unlocked the drawer and got out the address book."

Cranmer lit a Camel and stared at the wall. Finally he shrugged and said, "Zantell was blackmailing Taber."

"All my aunts are enterprising. What's the dirt?"

"Hell, she wouldn't say. Maybe you can turn something up in Ponca City. Zantell's from there too, so that'll give you something else to look for. You know anybody up there?"

"Naturally. I've got a buddy on the police force. Also a lady or two."

"Naturally. That insurance dick is following me around."

"What insurance dick?"

Cranmer remembered he hadn't talked to Maneri since the previous evening. He filled him in on Dreiser's visit.

"Seems odd he'd follow you," Maneri said.

"Yeah, it gives me a notion. Remember a flick called *Double Indemnity*?"

"Sure. It was just on television, right? Richard Crenna and Lee J. Cobb?"

"No, it's an old flick. Fred MacMurray and Edward G. Robinson. About an insurance salesman and a woman who insure her husband and then bump him off—throw him off a railroad train so they can collect double."

"That's the same movie I saw. Must have been a new version."

"Anyway, maybe that's why this Dreiser is so concerned. Could be he and Denise Taber set something up. Why don't you check and see who sold Taber his policy?"

"No problem. You couldn't get Kilduff into Solano, huh?"

"Nope. But this whole thing quit making sense when Rope said there were two killers. We haven't found two men yet who I can picture working together."

"Rope said they were both men?"

"Yeah. At least I think so. You'd better stay away from Zantell, Butch. Her studs seem to have a high mortality rate."

"I thought about that. Reckon there may be another jealous lover in the woodwork?"

"Anything's possible. Well, I'll let you go. Have fun in Ponca City."

"You know I will, dad. Hope nothing interrupts your football game. I don't suppose you got to watch the Series last night, did you?"

"Oh, I watched most of it over at Rope's while Bat Masterson was fumbling around. Say, I found that poker game tonight. Had to go over to Medwick, but it was worth the trip. A man wouldn't have to work in this area."

"Hell, you don't work much anyway."

"You haven't heard from Cindy, have you?"

"No such luck."

"Wish she'd hurry up with the financial dope on Kilduff."

"Hey, my damsel's stirring. Check you later."

"Don't bruise it."

Arnold Dreiser sat drowsily behind the wheel of his brown Malibu. The radio on the dashboard played a mournful tune by Conway Twitty. Dreiser tapped his fingers lazily on the steering wheel in approximate time to the music.

The club at the motel had emptied about an hour ago. Now the Solano Inn was dark and quiet. Dreiser had the frustrating intuition he was wasting his time. But if Cranmer was right about foul play, it would be a feather in his cap to save the company from paying the claim.

Trouble was, Cranmer didn't seem to be a particularly vigorous investigator. It hadn't been difficult for Dreiser to ascertain that Cranmer had spent over three hours playing poker in Medwick. Hell, an investigator had to get out and beat the pavements.

Dreiser lit a cigarette to stave off sleepiness. He had taken one drag when he saw the man approaching his car. Crap, he thought, some drunk saw the light. Probably wants to mooch a smoke. But the man seemed to walk steadily enough. And he was huge, even larger than Dreiser.

The man leaned up against Dreiser's car. "You're out late, friend," he said. He began to pop his knuckles, one at a time.

"Am I disturbing something?" said Dreiser.

"You got some identification?"

A cop, Dreiser thought. Should have known by his looks. He

arched a bit in the seat and reached for his back pocket. He had to turn slightly away from the man. Before he touched his wallet, he felt a viselike hand clamp over his throat.

Seven seconds seemed a long time to Dreiser.

Six

Richard Straight nudged the body carefully with his foot, and it tumbled down into the ditch. The body moved as tentatively as if its image had been captured with a slow-motion camera.

Straight walked back to the rented Dodge Dart on the shoulder of the road. Just in case, he limped heavily, favoring his right leg. He looked back at the ditch. Dreiser's corpse was not visible from the road.

He drove back to Solano. Once again he was thinly whistling Tchaikovsky. Something was out of kilter, he thought. It was the thirteenth job, and as feared, it was turning sour.

When he reached Solano, he looked for a phone booth. He found one outside a deserted gas station on Solano's Main Street. He gave the operator the New York number and readied coins in his hand.

August McEachern's voice was filled with sleep.

"This is Straight," said Straight.

"Hmmm. I trust this is urgent, Richard."

"It is to me. I want to know what the hell's going on."

"Time, for one thing. What did you have in mind?"

"This Taber job. It's getting more complicated all the time, and there's a rotten odor about it. We've taken out three people so far. Only one of them was necessary. If you'd let us clear out after Taber, there would have been no problem. And this Coady character you saddled me with is a complete, incompetent maniac. I want out of here. If you won't let me go, I want Coady out of here."

There was a pause. Then McEachern said, "Three?"

"Taber, the man who saw us kill Taber, and another man tonight, an insurance investigator. There's a cop on the job here I don't like. Guy named Cranmer. Used to be with the government and still is for all I know. He showed up at our hotel in Medwick tonight. He's tough. I worked with him before. I can't see anything to be gained by hanging around here."

"Botching a job doesn't permit you to simply disappear," McEachern said coldly. "You'll stay. And I told you why Coady's there. He's to stay also. Haven't you learned by now to clean up your own messes?"

Straight leaned his forehead against the cool glass of the telephone booth. After a moment he said, "Can you find out about Cranmer for me? First name Steve. I want to know if he's still a fed. Is there any reason for the feds to be in this?"

"Not that I'm aware of," said McEachern. "I'll check him out and let you know. And, Richard?"

"Yes."

"Next time you wet your pants, make it at a civilized hour, will you?"

McEachern hung up.

The old man closed his eyes, but sleep eluded him. Straight was sharp. He knew something was up, but he also knew what would happen if he disobeyed direct orders. What he didn't know was the same thing would happen even if he obeyed.

It was a dilemma. Coady didn't have the ability to improvise his way out of the Solano situation. So McEachern couldn't turn Coady loose on Straight until Straight settled things in Oklahoma. And the longer it took, the chancier it was. McEachern liked things smooth.

And Straight was leaving a lot of ragged edges.

Cranmer woke abruptly, with his knee throbbing as if a vibrator were attached to it.

He gazed at the ceiling for a moment, orienting himself, then slid his legs off the bed and let their momentum pull him into a sitting position. His cane was hooked on the bedstead. He picked it up and made his way slowly and painfully to the bathroom. There he unscrewed the lid of his pill bottle, shook two tablets into his hand, put them in his mouth, cupped a handful of water and washed the Demerol down, jerking his head back to get the tablets into his throat.

Cranmer watched his reflection in the mirror with disapprobation. When the reflection did nothing to surprise him, he limped back to the bed and lay on his back. Within half an hour the pills had relieved the throbbing in his knee. Then Cranmer shaved, dressed and went out for breakfast.

The brown Malibu was still in front of the Solano Inn. Cranmer glanced briefly at the adhesive tape on the driver's nose, then ignored his watchdog.

After a greasy breakfast, Cranmer returned to his motel room and read until time for the football game. At the end of the third quarter he was relaxed and starting to count his five hundred dollars. Tennessee had held Alabama to a 21–21 tie, and Cranmer was getting fifteen points.

Alabama's first touchdown of the last quarter didn't worry him. But when they scored again to take a fourteen-point lead, Cranmer swallowed a couple of Demerols.

He was sitting in the room's single chair, hunched forward and rooting hard when his door crashed open. Jamie Darden stood in the doorway. The .45-caliber pistol in his hand was aimed directly at Cranmer and it seemed as huge as a howitzer. "Don't you move, Cranmer," snarled the marshal.

Cranmer disconsolately returned his eyes to the television. Alabama had just scored again, a five-hundred-dollar touchdown.

It's going to be one of those days, Cranmer thought.

Maneri let the Fiat out. It had been a good Saturday, cool in the morning, warm in the afternoon. And he had found the secret in Arthur Taber's past.

He was listening to the radio rather than his tape player on his way back to Solano. The music wasn't much, but he was waiting for the football scores. Occasionally the disc jockeys interrupted to remind him Oakland had evened up the World Series at three games apiece and OU had trounced Colorado.

Finally the news came on and the football scores were announced. Maneri heard them and flashed them up in his mind as if on a giant movie screen.

Maryland 37, Wake Forest 0

Michigan 35, Wisconsin 6

Ohio State 37, Indiana 7

Penn State 49, Syracuse 6

Wonders never cease, Maneri thought. Four teams is ten to one, so that's two hundred dollars. Wait till Cranmer hears about that. And I gave away ninety-seven points.

Maneri switched off the radio and played tapes the rest of the way to Solano. He by-passed the town and took the back road to McIntosh Johnson's farm. Once again he secreted the Fiat in Johnson's garage.

Johnson came out to meet him. "Well, now," he said. "If it isn't my wandering employee. Nice trip?"

"Fair enough," said Maneri. "You busy feeding cows and chickens and llamas or can you run me into town?"

"I oughta run you out of town," Johnson said. "I've been getting quite a bit of static about hiring you ahead of some other people and then you only working half the time."

"You can bear up under it," Maneri said. "You've been county commissioner ever since Christ was a corporal; that should entitle you to something."

They climbed into Johnson's pickup, and Johnson drove Maneri to the Solano Inn. Maneri started to walk back to Cranmer's room and fill him in on Taber. Then he noticed the club was open. He decided to drink a beer first.

Darden kept the gun leveled on Cranmer and quietly closed the door to the motel room. Cranmer looked at him curiously. "Don't tell me you're the one who's been killing all of Solano's jewelers," he said skeptically.

"I'll ask the questions," Darden said importantly. "Where was you last night?"

"Why?"

"Because I wanta know. That's all the reason you need, Cranmer."

Cranmer shrugged. He reached out with his cane and stabbed

off the television. "I played cards in Medwick," he said resignedly. "You going to bust me for playing poker?"

Darden rubbed the toe of his right boot on his left pants leg. "You got some explaining to do, fellow, and you'd better make it plain. I'll do you a favor. I'll tell you what I know first."

"Terrific," said Cranmer.

"First off, you ain't with no insurance company. We checked you out. You're a private cop, but not with insurance. I also found out the real insurance cop's been in town. Guy named Arnold Dreiser. Know him?"

"We've met."

Darden nodded sagely. "That's good, Cranmer. You just keep on coming clean. According to the folks around here, you did a little more than just meet. They say there was a fight."

Cranmer shrugged. "If you could call it that."

"Doctor in town says Dreiser came out of it with a broken nose. There bad blood between you two?"

Cranmer looked at the marshal and waited.

"What time you get through playing cards?" Darden asked.

"Midnight. Maybe eleven-thirty."

"Hah! That's not late enough, Cranmer. Doc Keating puts it at about one A.M."

Cranmer sighed and nodded. "Dreiser's dead, huh?" he said.

"How you know that?" Darden demanded. "I ain't said nothing about nobody being dead."

"Yeah, that's a great old trick," Cranmer said. "You forget I was there last night at Rope's. I know Keating's the M.E."

"Oh." Darden was disconcerted momentarily. Then he recovered and said, "Funny how you're the only one that says Rope called you. All we really know is you was there alone with him and he ended up dead. Then Dreiser shows up and calls your hand, and he ends up dead. Both strangled. Doc Keating figures the same man did it for both of them. Man with a big hand."

"You say Dreiser was killed at one o'clock this morning?"

"That's right."

Cranmer remembered the brown Malibu in front of the motel when he went out for breakfast. "Did Dreiser have a bandage on his nose?" he asked.

"He did."

Cranmer wondered who in the hell had been following him. Had it been Dreiser last night and someone else this morning—the someone else most likely being Dreiser's killer? Or had Dreiser followed him at all? He wished he knew if the Malibu was still in front of the motel.

"Another thing we found," said Darden. "Tracks by the body. Tracks made by a man who limps. You got a quick explanation for that?"

"Not even a slow one," Cranmer said. "Looks like somebody's trying to hang this on me. You say you checked me out with Oklahoma City. Surely they didn't tell you I'm the kind of guy who goes around strangling people."

"The report we got said you're the kind of guy who goes around shooting people," Darden said. "But they did say you hadn't killed anyone."

"Why not put the cannon away?" Cranmer suggested.

Darden hesitated a moment, then holstered his .45. "I think it's time you come clean with me, Cranmer," he said. "You're a private cop in the City. That means you're working for somebody, right?"

"That's a fair assumption."

"Who?"

Cranmer lit a Camel and shook his head. "I can't tell you that, Darden. It's confidential; that's why I was using the insurance cover. You can make me tell you in court, but not anywhere else."

Darden scowled. "I think maybe I'd better take you in," he said. "You ain't exactly a model of cooperation."

Cranmer stood up and Darden jerked his .45 out of its holster and pointed it at him. "Relax, for Christ's sake," said Cranmer irritably. "I'm just going to the head. Sorry I didn't hold my hand up first."

Cranmer picked his cane up from beside the chair and limped into the bathroom. Darden watched him with narrowed eyes.

In the bathroom, Cranmer took a pair of Demerol tablets. If he had to go to jail, he could at least be comfortable. He returned to the main room and stepped into a pair of loafers.

Darden was watching him inquisitively. "Toss me your cane a minute, Cranmer," he said.

Cranmer glanced at him, startled, then flipped him the cane.

"Now walk over here," Darden instructed.

Cranmer looked at the ceiling beseechingly. Then he walked across the room to Darden, awkwardly dragging his right leg.

Darden handed his cane back to him. "That's what I was afraid of," he muttered.

Cranmer looked at him blankly.

"You really need that cane, don't you? It's not just an affec . . . something for looks."

"I really need it," Cranmer said patiently. "So?"

Darden reached down and removed a piece of lint from his boot. He sighed. "So sit down. You're not going any place."

Cranmer considered it for a moment, then said, "Problem with the tracks."

Darden seemed astonished. "You add things up fast," he said. "Yeah, it's the tracks. There wasn't no cane marks, just footprints. One lighter than the other. So we read a limp. Only you don't limp the right way. You drag your leg. Like this." He stood up and demonstrated Cranmer's walk. "So your track would be one deep footprint and then kind of a line where you dragged the other foot. That don't match what we've got."

Cranmer grinned at the marshal. "You are pretty good at this," he said, deadpan.

Darden shook his head sadly. "No, I'm in way over my head. Listen, Cranmer, I apologize for busting in on you like this. I really thought that, well . . ." He waved his hand to complete the sentence.

"Let's have a drink and talk about it," Cranmer suggested. He poured bourbon into glasses. "Water?" he asked.

"Neat," said Darden.

Cranmer filled his own glass with water and casually toasted the marshal.

"Not much goes on in Solano," Darden said. "Mostly I hand out tickets to people passing through. Sometimes I break up a fight. About the most trouble I've ever had is handling the kids who smoke pot. Now I've got three murders. I tell you the truth, I don't know where to begin. Wonder if I could ask you a favor, Cranmer. Not that I'd be surprised if you kicked me out on my can for the way I come in here. But this is your racket, right? You know how to investigate a murder?"

"I've handled some," Cranmer said.

Darden downed his drink and shuddered a bit. "If I just let you handle this in your own way, would you fill me in on what you find? Or could you give me any suggestions on what I should do?" Darden was embarrassed. His eyes did not quite meet Cranmer's.

"I can't promise to solve the damned thing," Cranmer said. "But I can tell you this: I don't want credit with anyone except my client. So if I latch onto a solution, I'll hand it to you."

"Thanks," Darden said, looking at the floor. "You got something I can do so I'll look like I know what the hell I'm doing?"

Cranmer lit another cigarette. "I suppose you've talked to all the people who live in Rope's apartment complex?"

"Yeah. Nobody saw nothing."

Cranmer nodded. "They hardly ever do. Well, Taber is the key to the whole thing. Why don't you concentrate on him? Find out all you can about his past, who might have a motive to kill him, things like that. That should keep you occupied for a while."

Darden stood up. "All right. Think I'll go talk to Denise first. I never did question her."

"Then she'd be a good place to start," Cranmer said. "You also might check the Taber neighborhood. Probably won't learn anything, but it's something that should be done."

"Right," Darden said efficiently. "You'll stay in touch?"

"I'll be around," Cranmer promised.

Darden started for the door, then turned abruptly and walked over to Cranmer. He extended his right hand. Cranmer kept his expression neutral and shook hands with the marshal.

"I thank you, Mr. Cranmer," Darden said officiously. Then the marshal strode from the room.

Cranmer flipped his cane onto the bed and walked to the television without dragging his right leg.

Hooray for Gene Autry, he thought.

. . .

"I love you, Butch," said Donald Dorne. "Anyone with red hair can't be all bad."

The newspaper reporter handed Maneri two one-hundred-dollar bills. "You seemed so damn confident, I went along with you," he said. "Put my twenty with your twenty and bet the forty on a four-team parlay. Broke my bookie's heart. It's the first parlay I've hit all year."

Maneri sipped Schlitz. "I hate to lower your opinion of me," he said, "but it's the first for me, too."

Dorne laughed. "Well, it couldn't have come at a better time. Tonight you drink on me."

"I might take you up on that later," Maneri said. "But I've got to see a man before I do any serious drinking tonight."

"All right. I'll be here. Say, how are you and Martha Henning coming along?"

"I may marry her," said Maneri.

"No."

"Well, no, but I don't think I'll throw her back for a while yet."

Maneri and Dorne drank beer for half an hour. The club was practically deserted at that hour.

Maneri downed his beer. "Gotta drift," he said. "Maybe we can shoot a little pool later."

"Only as partners. I've heard about your stick."

Maneri grinned. "Sometimes I get lucky." He left the bar and walked back to room number six. Before he knocked on the door, he put the two one-hundred-dollar bills and his stub from the parlay card in his hand. When Cranmer answered the door, he held them out to him.

Cranmer examined them sourly. "High School Harry strikes back," he said.

"Yeah," said Maneri. "Too bad about Tennessee."

"Oh, I came out all right," Cranmer said airily. "Texas and Air Force came through."

"So you made five hundred dollars?"

"Counting the juice, four hundred and fifty. But I won enough in that hokey poker game to support me for a while. Drink?"

"Nah, I'm on beer tonight."

"I nearly got arrested for murder today," Cranmer said.

Maneri laughed. "Who'd you kill?"

"The insurance investigator: Dreiser."

"Well, there goes the double-indemnity theory."

"Yeah. This damn case is making less sense all the time."

Cranmer filled Maneri in on Jamie Darden's visit. Then he said, "Did you make it to Ponca City today, or were you too busy humping the jewelry broad?"

"I'm hurt," said Maneri. "You know it's always duty first with me. Not only did I go to Ponca City, I think I found out what Tracy Zantell had on Taber."

"Good boy. The man had a past, huh?"

"He was a fence. Anyway, something approximating a fence. My copper friend said he was an expert at restyling stones. The thief dropped off a hot rock, and Taber redesigned it into a ring or a pendant or something. Disguised it so well it could pass the hot list. Word is, he was tired of the operation. That's why he came to this dump. And Aunt Tracy left Ponca City two days after Taber."

"What'd she do in Ponca City?"

"Same thing Martha Henning does in Solano."

"So she'd know about the fencing?"

"It's a good bet."

"Better than a four-team parlay," Cranmer said sourly. "Okay, I'll brace Zantell about it. In the meantime, I want you to start checking out this Dreiser character. Last night he was following me. He was driving a brown Chevy, a Malibu. At least I thought it was him. When I went out for breakfast this morning, he was parked out in front of the motel. Only it couldn't have been him because he was already dead. But whoever was in the car had plaster on his nose. That's why I figured it was Dreiser."

"You want me to find out who was in the car?"

"Correct."

"How?"

"Hell, if I knew how, I'd do it myself. Use your native intuition. And watch yourself. Odds are whoever was in the car killed Dreiser. And unless I'm far wrong, whoever killed Dreiser also killed Rope and Taber."

"And now he's following you."
"Seems like."
"Well, if he kills you, I'll try to catch him in the act. Then we'll have the thing solved."
"Terrific," Cranmer said. "See if you can get hold of Cindy. I want that financial report."
Maneri went to work with the phone. Cranmer poured himself another drink.
After a brief conversation Maneri hung up the phone. "She mailed it," he said.
"Terrific," said Cranmer. "That means we won't get it till Monday."
"Well, she remembered enough of it to give us an idea," Maneri said. "The man is broke. Owes money everywhere. And as an architect, he's from hunger. The Solano job was his first in a long time."
Cranmer considered it. "Still seems like stretching things to kill for twelve thousand dollars," he decided.
"Don't forget Denise Taber's money."
"Yeah. Shit, there's too many suspects around for my taste. Maybe Taber did slash his own throat—in a fit of depression over his unpopularity."
"And then rose from the grave to kill Rope."
"Natch. Oh well, you go ahead and party. Not much we can do till Monday. Then I'll talk to those businessmen on either side of Taber who were wanting to sell out. Archer and Tomas. Trouble is, I already know what they're going to say."
"They didn't like Taber."
"Yeah. Who did?"

"Hello, Richard," said August McEachern.
"Yeah?" Straight said.
"My, you sound surly. Where have you been? I've been calling all day."
"We've been busy. Piling up corpses so you can keep on playing whatever game it is you're playing."
"Now, Richard, there's no game. I'm simply trying to help you do a job. This Steve Cranmer you're so worried about is no longer with the government. I'm told he was crippled and

refused to take a desk job. Another romantic. He is currently operating as a private detective in Oklahoma City. I'd say your feeble attempt at setting up a suicide failed to fool anyone."

"Thanks for the information," Straight said coldly. He replaced the receiver gently, cutting off McEachern's voice.

Straight glared across the room at Coady. "Have you grown fond of that adhesive tape?" he snarled.

Coady looked surprised, then reached up and pulled the tape off his nose. "Jeeze, Spinoza, don't take it out on me," he said plaintively. "Is it my fault . . . ?"

"Keep packing," Straight ordered. "If Cranmer's that thick with the Solano law, they may be here any minute. He didn't go anywhere this morning, huh?"

"Just breakfast."

"Then he must know. If he was still investigating, he'd be out working, not hanging around his motel room. Only one cop showed up?"

"Yeah. John Wayne type with a big badge and a bigger gun."

"That's all we need," said Straight. "Cranmer and John Wayne."

"It was funny sittin' out there and watching the law crash in," Coady said. "Reminds me of a gig in New York. Target that time was a cop, but it was one of my first jobs and I pretty much blew it. That's when I was still on the long-distance routine, and I used—are you ready for this?—a bomb. Blew the shit out of the copper's car. Only trouble was, he wasn't in it. Anyway, there was law all around that time, too."

Straight carefully folded a shirt and set it in his suitcase. Then he said indifferently, "A bomb, huh? What'd you do, rig it to the ignition?"

"Yeah. You know, just like the movies."

"Who started the car?"

"The cop's wife. Man, it was a strange scene. It was time for the cop to go on shift, and there wasn't no reason for his wife to be in the car. Trouble with bombs is, they ain't too selective."

Straight latched his suitcase. "Guess I'll leave the hot plate for the next occupant," he said. "Who was the cop? I've done some jobs in New York; maybe I knew him."

Coady continued throwing unfolded clothes into a trunk.

"Hell, I can't remember his name, Spinoza. That's been a while ago. They done things different back then, though. After I hung around a few days, they told me to disappear and forget it. Not like this gig."

"Times change," Straight said impassively. He held the volume of Kierkegaard in his hand for a moment, examining the cover. Then he sighed and flipped the book into the wastebasket.

Coady looked surprised. "You just throw them things away?" he asked.

"I'm through with it," Straight said. "I think we're going to have to hit Cranmer, Ham."

Coady grinned hugely, interlaced his fingers and cracked his knuckles. "Now you're talking," he said.

Straight checked his .45 Colt and replaced it in his shoulder holster.

"Gonna carry heat again?" asked Coady.

Straight smiled thinly. "I plan to handle this job personally," he said.

Cranmer whistled tunelessly through his teeth as he once again rapped on Tracy Zantell's door. It was a bright Sunday morning and he felt good. The previous night had been ideal. No interruptions, no overdose. He had floated through a good sex book and topped off the evening with a visit from a black whore, courtesy of the motel. And the first thing in the morning he had called Wally in Oklahoma City and put $550 on the Dallas Cowboys. They were twelve-point favorites over the New York Giants, and the Giants had quarterback troubles. If Cranmer won his bet, it would make it a thousand-dollar weekend.

And his subconscious had fortuitously stumbled on a possible solution to the Solano murders.

Tracy pulled the door open. "Mr. Cranmer," she said without much warmth.

"Hello, Miss Zantell," Cranmer said. "Figured you were about due for a report."

"Come on in."

They settled into chairs in the living room. Cranmer tapped his cane on the floor and glanced about the room admiringly.

"You live well, Miss Zantell," he said. "I guess crime pays, after all. You still refuse to tell me what you had on Arthur Taber?"

"I don't see where it matters," she said.

Cranmer nodded. "Maybe not. But I want to prove I'm earning my money. You realize Butch and I have put in several days on this case. It's going to cost you something."

Tracy shrugged. "I said I'd pay. Who's this other man who died?"

Cranmer told her. Then he said, "Why don't you invite me for lunch, Miss Zantell? We can talk about stolen jewels."

Her expression didn't alter. "I usually have sandwiches on Sundays," she said.

"That'll be fine, as long as you have some bourbon to camouflage the taste," said Cranmer.

Tracy walked into the kitchen. Cranmer hobbled after her. She was wearing black pants with flared legs and a pink sweater. The view was interesting.

"We did a little checking in Ponca City," Cranmer told her as she pulled a jar of mayonnaise from the refrigerator. "Just to be thorough. You know what we found, don't you?"

"It all depends on where you looked," Tracy said. She lathered two pieces of bread. "I understand the man with the tamale cart pushes marijuana on the side."

"Yeah, well, we were a bit more interested in Taber's old jewelry store. He had an interesting staff, didn't he? And an even more interesting clientele."

"So you found out," Tracy said. "It's not necessary to play games."

"Yeah, but I'd like to hear it from you. After all, you're the client," Cranmer complained.

She handed him a sandwich. "All right. I worked for Art. He made most of his money illegally. Someone would steal a relatively famous jewel. Something that couldn't be fenced in its original condition. Art was a master at restyling the jewels so they couldn't be recognized. What made him so good was he could create jewelry that, although markedly different, was quite valuable in its own right."

"And you knew about it."

"I caught on after a while. He never told me, but there were simply too many scabrous customers for a reputable jewelry store. I did a little snooping and a little eavesdropping and learned what was really happening."

"So you put the bite on him," Cranmer said, munching on his sandwich.

"Gradually. It seems strange now, after I became so close to him, but you have to remember that at the time Art was only an employer to me. I dropped a few hints, and he raised my salary. He raised it too much. I didn't really have any proof, but the way he reacted to my hints convinced me."

"Then he came to Solano. Why?"

"He wanted out. Later he told me he was becoming afraid of the people he had to work with. Evidently there was quite a bit of pressure. He was afraid he'd accidentally ruin a stone and they'd think he kept it for himself. So he told them he was getting too old, that his hands weren't steady enough any more for such delicate work. And he cleared out."

"And you trailed him."

"And I trailed him."

Cranmer finished his sandwich, and Tracy refilled his drink. "Did Taber's wife know about it?" he asked.

"No. That's what caused part of their trouble. She didn't want to leave Ponca City, and she certainly didn't appreciate the drop in income. Art made good money in Solano, but nothing like he'd made before."

"And besides, he had to cough up a thousand a month for you. I don't suppose he explained that to his wife."

"I wouldn't think so."

They returned to the living room. Cranmer looked hopefully at the television set and said, "You got anything on tap for this afternoon?"

"Sunday's my day for lazing," she said. "Why?"

"You like football?"

"As long as I don't run out of wine. And I've got a good supply. Who's playing?"

"The Cowboys."

"And you want to watch it here?"

"Correct."

"It doesn't seem to me you spend a hell of a lot of time working on this case," Tracy protested.

Cranmer shrugged. "What can I do on a Sunday? Tomorrow I'll go see Archer and Tomas. I don't really think they're involved, but they could shed some light."

"Are you making any progress at all?"

"Sure. At least it's definitely a murder now. That's progress, isn't it?"

"I suppose."

Tracy went to the kitchen and returned with a glass of wine. She turned on the television and curled up on the floor in front of it. Cranmer wondered what would happen if he curled up beside her. Maneri hadn't seemed to have much trouble scoring. But then, Maneri never did.

Then the Cowboy game started, and Cranmer forgot about Tracy Zantell.

The telephone woke Maneri. He searched the bedside table for his watch, then found it on his wrist. It was just after 10 A.M.

He picked up the phone and said "Hello" into the transmitter. His fingers had decided it was too early to wake up, and he had trouble holding onto the phone.

"Butch? This is Martha. How about rolling out of the hay and taking me to church?"

That woke Maneri up. He hadn't been to church since his sister's marriage, and he didn't plan to start now. "Couldn't do it," he said. "I haven't got any clothes."

"You looked all right when we went to Medwick," Martha reminded him.

"Yeah, but those are dirty now, and I haven't got anything else. Listen, you go ahead and then why don't you come on over? Or do you have something else in the works?"

"No, I'll do it. Lunch?"

"Well, that's another problem. All I've got is milk and beer. Why don't you pick up some Colonel Chicken or something? We can eat lunch and then lick each other's fingers."

"Sounds delicious. I'll be there a little after twelve."

"You're a dream girl," Maneri said, and hung up.

His stomach was making its presence felt. Maneri went into the bathroom and got a stomach pill, then went to the kitchen and washed it down with milk. He drank the milk straight from the carton. The doctor had told him milk would soothe his stomach, especially when it was empty.

Maneri showered, dried himself with a towel that used to be white, and shaved. He was cheerful. He put the two one-hundred-dollar bills and his stub of the parlay card on the kitchen table where Martha could see them.

His feelings about the girl astonished him. The girls he knew didn't spend time with their parents and in churches. And Martha's restrained eroticism gave sex a whole new dimension.

Maneri donned a pair of jeans and a short-sleeved velour pullover. Then he sat in a chair by a window. The sun was shining, and the leaves on the trees were giving the first hint of their autumn colors. Kris Kristofferson's song about Sunday morning ran through Maneri's mind, and he wished he had his stereo in Solano.

Maneri's heart actually jumped when he saw Martha's car pull up in front of his rented house. He met her at the door, removed the bucket of chicken from her hands, then gave her a long kiss. "It's criminal for anyone to look so good in the mornings," he told her.

Her smile sent vibrations through the room. She was wearing a simple black dress with a high white collar and white cuffs on the sleeves.

Maneri kissed her again and lingeringly ran his hands over her body. She moaned a little, deep in her throat, and snuggled against him. "We'd better eat," she said.

"The chicken?"

She laughed richly. "For now," she said.

They walked into the kitchen. Maneri set the bucket of chicken on the table, grabbed a couple of plates and started looking for some silverware. "You're going to have to raid your jewelry store and get me some silver," he said.

Martha picked up the money and the parlay card. "You won," she said delightedly. "I listened to the scores yesterday, but I couldn't remember what your bets were."

"It's beautiful, isn't it?" said Maneri. "I can pick up that much almost any night shooting pool, but it's pleasant to do it through sheer luck."

Martha put chicken and mashed potatoes on the plates. Then she said, "Oh, I brought you something. I almost forgot. Stay right here."

Maneri sat down at the table. Martha went outdoors and returned in a minute, carrying a transistor radio. "You said you missed music," she said.

Maneri took the radio and turned it slowly in his hands.

"Don't you like it?" Martha asked worriedly.

Maneri was having a hard time with his emotions. He looked up at Martha and was afraid he might cry. "It's just that it's been a long time since anyone gave me anything," he said.

Martha put her arms around his neck, and he held her tightly for a moment. Then he broke the mood, saying, "We'd better make sure it operates. It might have been made in America by mistake."

He tuned in a rock station, and they started eating chicken.

Dallas made it a thousand-dollar weekend for Cranmer. Norm Snead kept Cranmer taking Demerol, but Dallas came out on top 45–28. Tracy had gone to bed at the half. She had consumed half a bottle of wine and wasn't concerned about maintaining her record as a good hostess.

Cranmer called a cab and rode to Denise Taber's. He was beginning to feel like a postman as he knocked on the door. The widow wasn't glad to see him. She blocked the door and said, "Your act failed, Mr. Cranmer. Or didn't the insurance company contact you?"

"Oh, I thought we might talk about Jeremiah Kilduff," said Cranmer.

Her eyes darkened, but she opened the door. Cranmer walked directly to the study and tried the locked drawer in the desk. It slid open easily. It was still empty.

Denise Taber glared at him from the doorway. "You still haven't produced a warrant, Mr. Cranmer," she said icily.

"Last time I was here this drawer was locked," Cranmer said. "I think it might be to your benefit to tell me what was in it."

"A body, what else?" She stalked into the living room.

Cranmer limped after her. "I suppose you heard about Dreiser," he said.

She lit a cigarette. "Who's Dreiser?"

"The insurance man they sent to check me out. Somebody killed him Friday night—Saturday morning, really."

"My God!" She stubbed out the cigarette. "That makes three people."

"You count well." Cranmer sat down, uninvited. Denise Taber sank down on the couch. "You know about Rope, don't you?" he asked.

She nodded.

"This is a dangerous town," Cranmer commented.

"Who are you, Mr. Cranmer? What's going on here?"

"I'm just a broken-down detective. What's going on here is called murder. Starting with your husband."

"I thought that might be what you were driving at. Jamie Darden was here yesterday evening, and he seemed to have changed his mind about Art. But he wouldn't say why. Do you know?"

Cranmer was trying to figure the lady out. When she talked about her husband, it was as though she were discussing a stranger. "Rope called me just before he got it," he said. "He said he had proof your husband was murdered. Said the people who did it had threatened him—and I guess they had. They made good on the threat before I had a chance to talk with him."

"If someone killed Art, it was Tracy Zantell," Denise said dogmatically. "She was here, wasn't she?"

"Funny," Cranmer said. "She says the same about you."

"Me? Why would I kill Art?"

"Kilduff?"

"Oh, come on, Mr. Cranmer. If you're a detective, you know there's nothing unusual about love affairs. It's certainly no cause for murder."

"Wouldn't be the first time."

She lit another cigarette. Then, speaking through exhaled smoke, she said, "Tracy was here, and I wasn't, Mr. Cranmer. If your snooping turned up the facts about me and Jerry, you know I was in Norman when Art died."

Cranmer shook his head. "No, ma'am. I know you were in Norman last Thursday, but I wasn't around to check you out the week before. You take pains to conceal your visits to Kilduff, don't you?"

She nodded thoughtfully.

"Then I doubt there'd be many witnesses to swear you were out of town. Kilduff might testify for you, but why would a jury believe your lover?"

"A jury!"

Cranmer gave what he hoped was a sinister nod.

"You're not serious! They're not really going to arrest me, are they?"

"I don't know, Mrs. Taber. You know more about Wyatt Earp than I do. Do you figure Darden's capable of seeing past the obvious?"

She mashed out the cigarette and immediately lit another. "I don't even think Jamie's capable of seeing the obvious. But surely, Mr. Cranmer, you don't think I could cut Art's throat and watch him bleed to death. No matter what you think of me, you couldn't think that."

Cranmer pointed his cane at her. "I'll level with you, Mrs. Taber. I don't think you were involved. But I need more than a feeling to give Darden. I think you should talk to me."

"I'm talking. What do you want to know?"

"Let's start with the drawer. What was kept in it that had to be locked up?"

Denise spread her hands helplessly. "I don't see how it could have any bearing. That's the drawer where Art kept his address book. I always had the feeling he associated with some unsavory characters, and I assumed he listed their names in the book and locked it up out of simple prudence. But I took the book out of the drawer the other day and read it. I didn't see anything dangerous or unusual about it. So I threw it away."

"And then locked the empty drawer."

"Did I?" She looked at Cranmer guilelessly.

"You did."

"Well, I don't recall that. I'm sorry. Perhaps it was habit."

Cranmer lifted his lip. "I don't like that part of your story,

Mrs. Taber," he said mildly. "What was in the address book that made you throw it away?"

"Nothing, I tell you. Most of the names I didn't even recognize."

"Was Tracy Zantell's name there?"

"Of course not," she said scornfully. "Art wasn't so old he'd forget his sweetheart's number."

"I thought you said they were just friends."

"I thought you said we were through kidding. Art had been having an affair with her for ages. She even followed us down here from Ponca City. Why do you think I started playing around?"

Cranmer shrugged. "I never claimed to understand women. Did your husband ever confide in you about his business dealings?"

"Only when he couldn't afford to buy me something."

Cranmer laughed. "Kilduff, of course, keeps you in mink."

"He keeps me warm with affection," Denise Taber said dramatically.

"Sure he does. How long have you two been sharing a blanket?"

"Maybe a year. We met at a council meeting when he outlined his plans for the courthouse."

"You didn't arrange for him to get the contract?"

"Certainly not."

"You know it's the first work he's had in a long time."

"That's because he's so innovative and creative. Most people are too stodgy to listen to his ideas."

Cranmer shook his head. "Well, I wish you happiness," he said sardonically. "Who else besides you had a motive to kill your husband?"

"I had no motive, Mr. Cranmer. Probably he threw Tracy out and she did it."

"Yeah, that makes sense. Then she called the cops because she didn't want the body to get cold lying there on the bathroom floor."

Denise stared at him vacantly. Then she said, "Detectives don't work for free, do they, Mr. Cranmer? Who hired you?"

"Orestes."

"Oh, shit," said Denise. "Why don't you go away, Mr. Cranmer."

"No suggestions on a motive, huh?"

"Just Tracy Zantell."

Cranmer hesitated a moment, then said, "You'd just as well forget that notion, Mrs. Taber. Your husband was paying the Zantell frail's bills. A grand a month. She wouldn't knock off the golden gander."

Denise Taber bristled. "That bitch!" she said.

Cranmer stood up. "Yeah, well," he said. "I'll keep in touch. Let me know if you change your mind about that address book. I'm at the Solano Inn."

"You haven't told me anything about the insurance investigator," Denise protested.

"He died," Cranmer said. "That's all I know."

He went to the phone and called a cab. As he waited by the front door, he asked Denise Taber about her plans concerning the jewelry store.

"Peter Brindle was here yesterday," she told him. "He was rather persuasive. I think I'll sell the damn thing to them. I may sell everything I have and move away from here."

"To Norman?"

"Well, what of it?"

A taxi parked in front of the house and beeped twice.

"Take care of my client," Cranmer said. "I think he likes liver best."

Maneri and Martha were sleeping on Maneri's bed, their bodies intertwined.

Maneri wasn't sure what woke him. But when he opened his eyes, he saw Gail Hand standing in the room. Her eyes were wide and frenzied. Her body sagged against the bedroom wall. Maneri couldn't think of an opening line.

"You son of a bitch," Gail said.

Maneri's grin was not the result of amusement. He removed his arm from beneath Martha's shoulders, and the jostling caused Martha to wake up. Her sleepy eyes looked from Gail to Maneri.

"Working!" said Gail with the sarcasm only a woman can manage. "A suicide, you said. Some suicide. Is this the corpse?" She indicated Martha.

Martha was as baffled as she was embarrassed. She said nothing.

"I don't recall inviting you down here," Maneri drawled.

"You son of a bitch," Gail repeated. "My little girl's out in the car."

Maneri shrugged. "If you'll wait outside for a while, I'll roll you a joint," he offered.

"You son of a bitch. I come all the way down here to see you —a nice surprise, I thought. It's a surprise, all right. I thought we had an understanding. I thought . . ."

"How'd you find the house?" Maneri asked politely.

Gail made a tiny fist and hit the wall with it. "You thought you were well hidden, huh? Well, the telephone operator gave me the address. Next time you leave town to shack up you'd better remember to do without a phone."

Maneri looked over at Martha. She refused to meet his eyes. Maneri's stomach was churning. He doubted either of the women would sympathize with him.

"Look, Gail," he said. "I don't mind you dropping in. But couldn't you at least let us get dressed before we have the big discussion?"

"This isn't a discussion, you son of a bitch . . ."

"You're repeating yourself," Maneri said, forcing a laugh.

"Oh, Butch, why?" She could no longer restrain her tears. She glared wordlessly at the pair in the bed as the tears ran down her cheeks. Then she turned and ran from the room.

"Jesus," Maneri muttered. He lit a cigarette.

Martha threw back the covers and climbed out of bed. Her entire body was pink from embarrassment. She began to dress.

"What are you doing?" Maneri asked.

"Leaving," she said shortly.

Maneri closed his eyes and blew smoke at the ceiling. "Look," he said, "she's just a friend. Or was. There's no ties between us."

"She said you were here to investigate a suicide," Martha said, stepping into her slip. "That means Mr. Taber. You've been using me."

"Now that's not . . ."

"You're cold, Butch. You're empty. You frightened me the night you beat up Clark. But I could live with that. I told myself Clark picked the fight and deserved whatever he got. But inside I could tell you enjoyed it. You enjoyed hurting him. I don't know what you really do, but it's something that makes you take pleasure from hurting people. And I've never seen that girl before, but she made my heart ache." Martha zipped her dress and turned to face Maneri. "And you laughed at her."

"Well, goddamn," Maneri said. "Can I help it if she storms in here? I bet I'm not the first man in your life. Did I get mad at you because of that clown Clark?"

"You were probably glad of the opportunity to prove how tough you are," Martha said.

Maneri laughed. "Jesus Christ," he said. "You women sure stick together."

"Most people do, Butch. You might contemplate that."

"Go on, get out of here," Maneri said.

Martha walked rigidly from the room. Maneri viciously stabbed his cigarette in the ashtray. Then he got out of bed and went to the kitchen to roll a joint.

The transistor radio was still on the kitchen table. Maneri smoked the joint with his right hand. His left hand absently caressed the radio. His eyes looked as if a translucent shield were covering them—keeping the world out and the emotions in.

Cranmer set his left foot just behind the service line, flipped the yellow ball into the air, bent his knees and arched his back, then drove the racquet into the ball with a powerful overhand motion. The ball raced across the court and hopped off the white line.

The opponent returned the ball by blocking it back. Cranmer had followed the momentum of his serve to the net. He took three catlike steps to his left and volleyed the ball back across the net, away from the opponent. But the opponent reached it and arched a high lob. The ball rotated slowly in the air. Cranmer could see the seams. He waited; then, leaping into the air, he smashed an overhead winner.

Now it was match point.

Cranmer's bronzed body gleamed with sweat. It contrasted nicely with his white tennis outfit.

Once again Cranmer positioned his feet and flipped the ball into the air. But when the ball collided with his racquet, it exploded and began to scream. The opponent was gone and Cranmer was alone on the court with the screaming. He could not find the source of the scream. He began to run, his powerful legs eating up the ground. Cranmer ran through an alien countryside.

He realized he was in Portugal. But there were no people in Portugal and he continued to force his legs forward in his solitary race against the scream. Then he saw he was approaching an enormous sand dune. The dune shifted in the bright sunlight.

Suddenly Cranmer's powerful running ceased. He realized his cane was in his hand, and his right knee was gone. There was only an empty space where the knee should have been. Below the vacant space, Cranmer's calf and foot continued to function independently.

Cranmer recognized the screaming now. It was his own voice, and it rose higher and higher as the tentacles of the sand dune grew longer and longer and came closer and closer to Cranmer's body, which was now incapable of flight. What confused Cranmer was he had been running toward the sand dune instead of away from it.

Cranmer jerked his eyes open before the sand could reach him. The sheet he was lying on was soaked with sweat, and his blanket was twisted about him so tightly as to render him almost incapable of movement.

He extricated himself from the blanket and sat on the edge of the bed. His right knee was burning. It felt as if an avalanche were occurring inside it. Cranmer thought he could almost see movement in the knee, as if small boulders were ricocheting off one another and stretching the skin.

"It must be this goddamn town," Cranmer muttered aloud.

He went to the bathroom for Demerol.

Half an hour later the imaginary avalanche had ceased, and

Cranmer could feel only the gentle throbbing with which the knee constantly reminded him of its presence.

Cranmer lay on his back on the bed and chain-smoked Camels, planning his day. Finally he picked up the telephone and called Wally in Oklahoma City. "Well, have I broken your book yet?" he asked.

"You didn't do as much damage as the local fans," Wally told him. "Any week both OU and OSU beat the point spread, I'm in trouble. But the Eagles made up for it yesterday. Nobody figured they could stay that close to the Vikings."

"Yeah. Gabriel's made them pretty tough. What's the line on tonight's game?"

"Let's see." There was a pause while Wally got his sheet. "Oakland's playing Denver, at Denver, and giving five points."

"Oakland minus five?"

"Right."

"Hmmm. I figured it would be more. Wouldn't surprise me a lot if Denver beat them. At five points, I don't guess it would surprise the odds-makers much, either, huh?"

"Guess so."

"Well, I've had a good week up to now," Cranmer said. "I think I'll just bet enough to make the game interesting to watch. Let me have two and a half on Denver."

"Denver, two hundred and fifty dollars. You've got it."

"Hold onto my money for me. God knows when I'm going to get back home."

Cranmer replaced the telephone, then, reluctantly, dressed and went out to talk to Archer and Tomas. He also wanted to talk to Solano's version of a lawman, Jamie Darden.

Richard Straight and Hamilton Coady were parked across the street from the Solano Inn. Room six was visible from their position. Their vehicle now was a green Mustang.

Straight sat in the passenger's seat, his mind totally blank. He had decided what must be done, and he had determined the method. Now it was simply a matter of timing.

It was nearly noon when Cranmer emerged from his room at the Solano Inn. He was wearing a maroon turtleneck sweater, and he limped heavily. Straight wondered obscurely what had happened to his leg. When they had worked together before, in New York, Cranmer had been quite a physical specimen.

Times change, Straight thought. Now we're both cripples.

"We gonna follow him?" Coady asked, reaching for the key in the ignition.

"No," Straight said quietly. "Let's wait in his room."

Coady shrugged and cracked his knuckles. "Wish this goddamn job would end," he said.

"Soon it will," Straight told him.

Cranmer permitted barber Anthony Tomas to administer an unneeded haircut. The main subject of discussion in Tomas' barbershop was the sudden rash of killings in Solano.

Cranmer, playing the out-of-town stranger, eventually managed to change the subject. "Whatever happened to the new courthouse?" he asked. "Last time I came through Solano, that's all anyone was talking about."

Tomas stropped his razor, then went to work around Cranmer's ears. "Something come up," he said resignedly. "Something always does."

"What happened?"

"Hell, I don't know for sure. I'm all ready to sell this joint to the government or whoever, but the man next door, Taber"—Tomas waved his razor in the direction of the jewelry store—"got the shaft put to him some way. I think they tried to cheat him out of his building. Anyway, he said he wouldn't sell it to them. And without his building, the whole thing collapsed. That's the trouble with this town—they give up too easy."

"You mean this guy next door kept you from selling out?" Cranmer asked.

"Nope. Weren't his fault. It's that goddamned government, always trying to get something for nothing. They made me a fair offer, but that's probably only because my place ain't worth as much as Taber's. You know he's one of the guys that got killed here?"

Back to the murders. Cranmer sighed. As he paid for the haircut he said to Tomas, "Well, it's too bad you couldn't retire."

"No sweat," said the barber. He waved his hand vaguely

around the one-chair barbershop. "I don't really mind coming down here. I don't actually cut that much hair. Even if I'd sold the place, I'd probably be down on a bench outside the new courthouse shooting the breeze every day anyway. Ain't gonna hurt me none to shoot it here instead of there."

Cranmer walked out of the shop. And Zantell pictured Tomas as a killer. Hell, the old man didn't even understand what was going on.

Cranmer went past Taber's jewelry store and into Archer's Tavern. It was brightly lit, as taverns go. There was a narrow bar with high stools running along one wall. Two of the stools were occupied, and one man was sitting behind the bar. A shuffleboard table ran down the center of the room, but it was not in use. At the back of the bar was a folding table surrounded by half a dozen folding chairs. Old men sat around the table playing dominoes.

Cranmer walked to the bar, hoisted himself onto one of the high stools and ordered a draft. The man behind the bar served him, then extended his right hand. "Haven't seen you in here before, mister," he said. "My name's Sam Archer. I run the place."

"Cranmer," said Cranmer, taking the proffered hand. "I was just driving through and got thirsty."

"Yeah," Archer said. "A man can get thirsty even when it's cool, can't he? Good thing, too, or I'd have to close up like them drive-in movies."

Cranmer nodded and sipped his beer. "Figured the next time I came through Solano they'd at least have that new courthouse started," he said. "That's all everyone was talking about last time I came through. What's the holdup? Having trouble getting steel? I know there's a shortage there."

Archer shook his head disgustedly. "The whole thing went down the drain," he said.

"Yeah? What happened?"

"Beats me. City council fucked up the money some way. There was one guy who wouldn't sell his property to them, and they just give up. Shit," Archer snorted. He rapped his fist on the bar. "Man's gotta be able to horse trade to get anything done in this world," he said. "You can't give it up just 'cause everything don't go like you had it planned out. Man's gotta be able to im . . . impor . . . What the hell's the word?"

"Improvise?"

"Right. Man's gotta be able to improvise. 'Specially in gov'ment dealings. You think them folks in Congress up there in Washington give up every time they run into a little hassle?"

Cranmer shrugged.

"Damn right they don't," Archer said emphatically. "They wheel and deal. Man from Arkansas kisses the man's ass from Oklahoma—or versa vice usually 'cause Oklahoma's got most of the ass kissers—and they trade a favor here for a favor there and work out their problems. Maybe not the way they wanted in the first place, but at least they get something done. I tell you, next election's gonna see some new faces around here."

"You were going to sell your place, weren't you?" asked Cranmer.

"Yeah, but I was just gonna move across the street. Don't know what the hell I'd do with myself if I didn't have this place to come to every day. Why else get up in the morning?"

"Man needs a reason," Cranmer said, and swallowed the last of his beer.

"Need another?" asked Archer.

Cranmer shook his head. "Better get back on the road," he said. "Quotas to make."

"Yeah, that's rough," Archer said. "Man, you couldn't pay me to work for somebody. This here place is my baby, and if I wanta spank it one day and leave it shut, there ain't nobody gonna tell me not to do it."

"Great work if you can get it," Cranmer said. He laid a dollar bill on the counter. "Keep it."

"Say, thanks, mister. You come back, now."

Cranmer limped out of the quiet tavern. Bet Maneri hasn't hit that place, he thought.

He went across the street to the marshal's office. Darden was there with the sheriff, Santo, playing gin rummy. Both men were wearing their cowboy hats. Santo was wearing a brown work shirt with a sheriff's badge pinned to it. Darden wore the traditional string tie, with an expensive-looking turquoise clasp. Neither man appeared to be upsetting his metabolism by investigating murders.

Darden riffled the cards and peered at Cranmer affably. "Mr. Cranmer," he pronounced. "You got something for us?"

Cranmer sat in a straight chair and hooked his cane over the arm. "Hello, Darden," he said. "Santo."

Darden dealt each man seven cards.

"We might talk a spell," Cranmer said with an affected drawl.

"I'm all ears," Darden told him.

Santo snorted. "That's about right," he agreed.

"Let's get a cup of coffee," Cranmer suggested, speaking to Darden.

Santo bristled immediately. "If you folks want me out of the way, I'll be glad to make myself scarce," said the sheriff. "Wouldn't want to come between a man and his only suspect."

Cranmer decided he didn't need any lawman, regardless of his capability, mad at him. "I want some coffee," he told Santo. "That's all I meant."

Santo nodded grudgingly. "You two go ahead. I'll stay and mind the store."

Darden rose from the card table and checked his appearance in the mirror. He straightened his voluminous hat and adjusted the turquoise clasp. Then, as Cranmer gaped at him, he leaned close to the mirror and mashed a pimple between meaty fingers. He wiped the juice from the sore on his pants.

"All set," he proclaimed.

Cranmer resisted the impulse to comb his newly butchered hair, and he and the marshal walked to a nearby café. Cranmer favored his right leg more than usual. After a waitress brought cups of weak coffee, Darden leaned forward confidentially and said, "I talked to Mrs. Taber after I left your place Saturday. That's a fine-looking woman. She couldn't tell me nothing, though."

Considering Darden's interrogation technique, that revelation failed to astonish Cranmer. He sipped the watery coffee, made a face at the cup and said, "If you can fit it into your schedule, I think it might be worth your while to drift over to Medwick today."

"Medwick? What would I be doing over there?"

Cranmer told him.

"Well," said the marshal, flicking an imaginary speck of dust off his prominently displayed holster, "I guess I can always charge the county a little mileage. Santo really ought to go—it's his territory."

"Yeah, but it's your case," Cranmer reminded him.

"So it is," Darden said sourly. "You come up with anything concrete yet?"

"Maybe we'll know that when you get back from Medwick," Cranmer said patiently.

"Right." Darden stood up importantly and remained beside the booth for a moment, allowing the few patrons of the café the opportunity to view his splendor. Then he said, "Don't worry about the coffee. They won't charge me for it." He strode out of the café.

Cranmer laid two quarters on the counter, and the waitress looked at him in surprise. "Christmas comes but once a year," he said vaguely. He figured he'd done enough work for one day. He'd wait for the marshal's report in his motel room.

Straight allowed Cranmer ten minutes to clear the area. Then he and Coady left the Mustang and walked back to unit number six of the Solano Inn. Locks on motel doors are notoriously vulnerable. The pair of killers was inside the room in less time than it would take the average person to extricate his key from his pocket.

No disguises were in evidence. Straight had not even brought his attaché case with the Encyclopaedia Britannica sales information. And the auburn wig had joined Kierkegaard in the trash basket.

When they were settled in the room, Coady asked about the lack of subterfuge.

Straight shrugged his slender shoulders. "We've passed that point," he said obscurely.

Coady seemed satisfied. He assumed his post at the window. "This reminds me of a job I done once in Corpus," he began.

Straight cut him off. "Coady, did it ever occur to you that the history of your colorful existence holds remarkably little interest for me?"

"Just makin' conversation," Coady said, hurt.

"Converse with yourself," Straight told him. "That way you'll have an interested audience."

Coady peered out the window and began popping his knuckles against the windowsill.

Straight turned on the radio in the wall of the motel room. A twangy guitar competed with a nasal voice. Straight searched for the station he had been listening to in Medwick and was eventually rewarded with a Chopin prelude. Sitting on the edge of the bed, Straight remembered the way Jill would curl up on the floor in front of the phonograph and let the music wash over her like waves on a beach.

Straight was wearing his best black suit, an outmoded white shirt and a wide black tie. He had spent nearly half an hour the previous night brushing a high sheen onto his black shoes. The white shirt had French cuffs, and he had secured them with a pair of solid-gold cuff links which bore a delicate design which could be interpreted as a policeman's badge. The cuff links had been a present from his wife. He had not worn them for years.

Coady continued to stare sulkily out the window.

Straight crossed his legs carefully and waited patiently on the bed. The motel room was cheap, both in appearance and atmosphere. It looked like a room that should be rented by the hour. A place for moldy love affairs or a quick shot of H. Cranmer's stay had obviously left no traces of his personality. Living out of a suitcase, Straight thought.

He wondered why Cranmer hadn't turned them in to the law. Coincidence was not a principle he believed in. Cranmer must have traced them to the Medwick hotel. How, Straight couldn't imagine. But he knew it was the unimaginable that proved the downfall of the intellectual criminal.

A man who walked into a store with a gun and escaped with a handful of change should never be astonished when he heard the ominous pounding on the door. What else could he expect? Assuming the ignorant had expectations. Which, of course, they did. The question was whether they were realistic assessments or mindless dreams.

But the man who figured the angles, the geometrician, had to remain constantly aware of the irrationality of mathematics. It was perhaps a mathematical law that the angles of a plane triangle would always total 180 degrees. The problem was that what appeared to Straight to be an isosceles triangle might assume the form of a scalene triangle in the mind of a man like Cranmer. Coupled with that was the bothersome possibility of a spherical triangle, in which the degrees could total 540.

Straight tried to clear his mind. After all, it made no difference.

The radio switched from the tinkling of Chopin to a deep resonant voice hustling pizza. Then the voice—which probably belonged to a man five feet two with thick glasses and an acne problem—announced the concert special of the day: an uninterrupted rendition of Tchaikovsky's Fourth Symphony. Almost perfect, Straight thought.

When the music crashed into the room with its initial burst of monumental authority, Coady jerked about convulsively and stared at the wall radio. "Jeeze, Spinoza," he complained. "Cranmer can hear that son of a bitch from six blocks off. You want him to know we're waiting in here?"

Straight stared at Coady wordlessly. After a moment Coady returned to his vigil at the window.

The thirteenth job, Straight thought. The thirteenth job, and a black cat to boot. But the fourteenth will be easier. A man should take pleasure in his work.

He tried to occupy his mind with the attempt to recall the faces of the dead. Because if his concentration slipped, his vagrant and masochistic thoughts raced back through time and tormented him with a picture of his wife's body decorating the wall of his garage like a modern painting. For years he had successfully blanked out the picture.

There was no kitchen equipment in the motel room. Straight went into the bathroom and turned on the hot-water tap. He watched the stranger in the mirror as the water heated. When it had reached its maximum temperature, Straight filled a glass with the water and went back to sit on the bed. He sipped the water and listened to the music.

Coady turned from the window to watch Straight and shook

his head in disgust. "We may be here all day, Spinoza," he lamented. "Ain't no way to know when Cranmer's comin' back. Or if he'll be alone."

"It doesn't matter, Coady," Straight said impassively.

The first movement of the symphony concluded.

Straight sipped his hot water. It was slightly discolored, as if someone had been using it for a chemical test.

"This is worse than waiting for that Rope character," Coady commented. "At least we knew about what time he'd show up."

"You aren't nervous, are you, Coady? I thought you had nerves of steel," Straight said derisively.

"Just got ants in my pants. I don't like this winging it. I'm a man to take orders."

"You want an order?"

"Yeh, if you happen to have one handy."

"Then shut up and keep looking."

"Goddamn if you ain't a cheerful soul," Coady said, but he turned back to the window.

Straight hummed absently along with the radio, but his mind finally returned to the present. There was something offbeat about Coady. Why had he gone into the Taber house? His instructions had been to honk if someone appeared. And Rope had said he saw Coady come out of the house, not enter it. Straight had decided Coady had failed to honk the warning because he had been inside the house when Rope arrived. But he could think of no logical explanation for that.

Coady stiffened by the window. "Here comes the man," he announced. "Just hobblin' down the street. All he needs is a tin cup."

Straight meticulously set the glass of water on the bedside table. He removed the .45 Colt from his shoulder holster and checked to insure its readiness.

Then he pointed the pistol negligently at the door.

Seven

Maneri's mood had improved substantially, primarily because he was working hard enough to keep his mind off women.

The road crew was resurfacing 1.8 miles of blacktop which had been decimated by torrential downpours. It wasn't Maneri's idea of the perfect way to spend a day, but it kept him occupied.

Maneri was sharing lunch with Jerry Blefary when he saw Donald Dorne's white MG approaching. Dorne parked the car and signaled Maneri to come over. Maneri climbed into the passenger's seat.

"You've been stringing me, Butch," Dorne said with no preliminary.

Maneri put an expression of polite curiosity on his face.

"I've been doing a little checking," Dorne said. "On my own, of course, because the boss still wants to play down these killings. But when I found out Steve Cranmer wasn't the insurance investigator he claimed to be, I called a contact of mine in the City. He filled me in on Cranmer. Also told me Cranmer worked with a guy named Maneri."

Dorne waited expectantly.

"So?" said Maneri.

"Well, hell, it's true, isn't it?"

"It's true."

"So why not give me a break? I can turn this into a hell of a story. It could be all I need to get out of this hick area and onto a good metropolitan newspaper."

"I didn't know there were any good metropolitan newspapers," Maneri said.

"Come on, be serious. What's the story?"

"You're not a dummy," Maneri said with annoyance, "you must have figured most of it out. Why brace me?"

"Look, Butch, don't take it that way. I'm not bracing you. I'm mainly after confirmation and a source. I can't just write what I *think's* been going on, you know that. But if you'd give me an interview, it'd help me a lot—and it would give your agency some good publicity."

"We're turning down work now," Maneri said petulantly. "You blast a story like that on page one, and every crank in the state's going to be after us. This case was unusual. It really wasn't what it seemed. But most of them are. Most deaths that look like suicides *are* suicides. Besides, it's not my place to give you an interview—even if I agreed with the principle."

Dorne rubbed his eyes and tried to think up a new approach. Maneri lit a cigarette and blew smoke through the car window.

Finally Dorne said, "Will you at least listen to my theory of things and confirm it if it's right? Or tell me where I'm off? Not for the newspaper, damnit, but to satisfy my bloodhound instinct. Although, God knows it would make a fantastic feature story: an undercover agent right here in Solano, working for the county during the days, roaming the town at night pumping people for information about the Taber murder—people being pumped, including the reporter who could write the story, but I don't hold that against you, Butch, I think it's fantastic—even dating an employee of the murdered man. Jesus, Butch, I'd just like to know how you got into the picture so fast. You'd make a hell of a newspaper reporter yourself. It took me damn near a year to win these country folk over, win their confidence enough so they'd talk to me. You've accomplished as much in five days as I did in a year."

Maneri laughed at him. "Flattery will get you nowhere," he drawled. "Maybe you're a commonplace reporter. Let me hear your theories, and I'll decide."

"All right," said Dorne. "You and Cranmer run a detective agency. That means someone hired you to come down here. Right? You're not philanthropists. Or, as Senator Ervin would say, your agency is not an eleemosynary institution. So you have a client. Wouldn't care to tell me who, would you?"

"I'm not the Oracle of Delphi."

"More like the Sphinx," Dorne complained. "Okay, you've got a client, Mr. X. He doesn't buy the story Taber slashed his own throat, and he convinces you there's a good chance he's right. So you and Cranmer burst into action. Cranmer hits town openly, questioning everyone involved—no matter how remote the connection. Hell, I heard about him the first day he was here. Talking to the mayor, the city manager, Taber's widow—all under the masquerade as an insurance investigator who distrusted suicides when there's a big payoff involved.

"You're the undercover half of the team. I admit I have no idea how you wangled a job with the county. But I guess that's your profession and you know how to go about it. As far as I can tell, your half of the job is to float around Solano, picking up stray information. Since you're aware of the entire situation, a chance remark dropped by someone who didn't know who you were could give you a hint—a clue. That's why you spend so much time in bars: to listen to the drunks gossip. And there's not much to gossip about in this town except Art Taber and the apocryphal courthouse. And you're good with women. There's a lot of folks who've been trying to get to first base—or even to bat—with Martha Henning. Or did you take her into your confidence? I imagine she'd be quite eager to help you nail whoever killed her boss."

"I don't take anybody into my confidence," Maneri said bluntly.

"Then you're good with women. Now, that much is pretty well cut and dried. I've got to start guessing now, because I don't have any idea what you and Cranmer found out. Whatever it was, it got Michael Rope killed Thursday night. Of course, we played it way down in the paper. Rope was a fairly prominent citizen, and heaven forbid we should step on any toes simply for the sake of accurate reporting. But the story I got is Rope called Cranmer and told him he had the goods on whoever killed Taber. So if there was any question left about a possible suicide, that axed it. But Cranmer says Rope was dead when he got there.

"Now, my source in the City says Cranmer's not above lying to the law when it will serve his purpose. But I can't see any purpose here, unless he killed Rope. And I have to admit that's a far-fetched notion, even for me."

Maneri lit another cigarette. "Cranmer carries a gun," he said whimsically.

"Yeah, so does Jamie Earp. Anyway, nobody suspects Cranmer. He goes back to the motel, has a row with the real insurance investigator, Dreiser, and Dreiser ends up in a ditch the next day with his throat mashed the same way Rope's was. Taber got it in the throat too, didn't he? So I think all three murders are related, sequentially, and I think Darden's hoping to hell Cranmer isn't his killer and will be able to solve it for him.

"I haven't been able to determine where you went this weekend," Dorne complained. "So I don't know if you added any information or not. But I figure it this way: someone bumped Taber, for whatever reason. Rope figured it out, and the same cat that did in Taber got Mike. That means it has to be someone local, right? Else Rope couldn't have cottoned on to it. What throws me is Dreiser. I can't make him fit in anywhere. Does it sound all right up to now?"

"You have an inventive mind," Maneri told him. "You don't really expect me to confirm anything for you, do you?"

Dorne hit the steering wheel with his fist. "Well, why the hell not? I can't print it without a source. What's wrong with satisfying my curiosity?"

"The main thing is we haven't broken the case yet," Maneri told him. "For all I know, you're the killer, and you're pumping me to find out if we're closing in on you."

"Oh, come on," Dorne said disgustedly. "I simply report things; I don't participate."

Maneri shrugged.

Dorne said, with an edge in his voice, "You know I could print a story revealing who you and Cranmer really are. I've got a source for that: the man in Oklahoma City."

"Did you ask him if he wanted to be quoted?"

"Hell, it doesn't make any difference," Dorne said, disgruntled. "I wouldn't do it to you. I like you. I wish you could clear the damn thing up." He peered through the windshield wistfully, as if visions of an AP byline were dissipating in his mind. "I'm not going to blow your cover, Butch," he said. "But remember, if I could find out, somebody else could, too. Take care."

Maneri felt an unwanted surge of sympathy for the young reporter. Maneri, too, had had dreams shattered. "Listen, Don," he said. "I can't promise anything—not right now. But why don't you go talk to Cranmer? He's already hit the papers on the Rope thing. If you catch him in the right mood, he might give you a story. The odds are against it; he's fairly intractable. But there's always a chance. I haven't spoken with him lately—could be he'd think a little publicity might help him."

Dorne grinned. "I'll try him," he said. "Thanks, Butch. Uh, one other thing. When you break it, will you let me have it? The *Oklahoman* won't do anything but have their state man call down here once in a while. And if it's solved, my editor won't mind giving the story the play it deserves."

"It's yours if we break it," Maneri promised. "After all, I'm still grateful for that parlay."

"Great!" Dorne extended his hand, and Maneri, grinning a little inside, shook it to seal the bargain. Maneri climbed out of the little sports car. Dorne revved the engine and sprayed gravel about as he headed for Solano.

Maneri had to laugh as he envisioned Cranmer's reaction.

"You'd better move away from the window, Coady," Straight said. "Wouldn't want to tip him off."

"Yeah," Coady mumbled. "You want I should go into the bathroom and cover you?"

Straight shook his head and smiled almost gently. "Why don't you sit down?" he said.

Coady lowered his bulk into the chair, which was facing the bed. He began to crack his knuckles one at a time.

"How do you think he feels right now?" Straight asked.

Coady looked surprised. "Cranmer? Beats the shit out of me. He don't know what's comin', so I guess he feels about the way he always does."

Straight's thin face seemed drawn. "What do you think it feels like, Coady, knowing you're going to die?"

Coady shrugged nervously. "What's the point of all this palaver, Spinoza? Everybody dies."

"Yes, everybody dies. Only some of us have the opportunity to see it coming."

"You mean you ain't gonna shoot him as soon as he comes through the door. You gonna play with him a little first?"

"I haven't made up my mind about Cranmer yet," Straight said. "But I think you'd make an amusing toy."

It took a long moment for Straight's comment to penetrate. Then comprehension slowly filled Coady's eyes and he stared helplessly at Straight. "Jesus, Spinoza," he rumbled throatily. "How'd you find out I was gonna hit you?"

Straight's .45 was leveled at Coady's heart. The pistol remained immobile. Only Straight's eyebrows arched a bit at Coady's statement. "Tell me about it, Ham," he said quietly.

"Well, goddamn, Spinoza, I don't know nothing about it. It was just an assignment, that's all. You'd've done the same thing in my place."

Straight's smile held a trace of amusement. "So Taber was my target, and I was your target," he said. "That's why they sent you along. I've never been able to understand that. Is that why you left the car and went into the Taber house?"

"Yeh, that's it," Coady said frantically. "I was going to hit you right after you hit the Okie." His eyes turned crafty. "But I couldn't do it, see, Spinoza? I got to where I liked you. Hell, I never done nothing to you, did I? I left the house 'cause I couldn't bring myself to do it."

Straight shook his head. "You left the house because the woman showed up and spoiled your plans," he contradicted. "I don't imagine they told you why I was being hit? No, they never explain, do they? Merely say kill this man or this woman—or this cop or this cop's wife—and never say why. Tell me how it feels, Coady, sitting there knowing you're going to die."

Coady watched him blankly.

"You make a poor subject, Coady," Straight told him. "It requires emotion, or even intellect, to fear death. You seem to lack both qualities. Speaking for myself, I find the notion of death quite restful. You want to hear something ironic, Coady? Something 'funny,' in your language?"

Coady's shoulders twitched.

"I didn't know you had me set up," Straight mused. "I thought there was something odd about your behavior, but then you're an odd sort of fellow. Remember the story you told me about one of your jobs? You must have told half a dozen—you're a man who likes to talk—but only one of them interested me. Remember the cop you were supposed to hit in New York? I believe you said it was one of your first jobs?"

"I can still take you, Spinoza," Coady snarled. "Seven seconds, remember?"

Straight made a slight motion with the pistol. "This is a .45-caliber, friend," he said softly. "You move off that chair, and even if I miss my aim and don't hit a vital spot, the impact will knock you back against the wall. I could bounce you off the wall all day. You've got strong hands, Coady, but they aren't .45-caliber."

Coady's eyes closed and he braced his body in the chair. He knew what a .45 would do.

"Now," Straight said impassively. "Do you remember the Mother Goose story about the cop in New York?"

"What the fuck is this?" Coady demanded. "Do it and get it done with!"

Straight smiled at him. It was a malevolent smile, tinged with joy. "Perhaps I've misjudged you, Coady. You do seem capable of fear. Good. I'd hate to believe it didn't worry you. After all, you killed me slowly for years. The least I can do in return is let you suffer a few minutes."

Fear, consternation and bafflement mingled on Coady's face.

"You set up a cop in New York," Straight said professorially. "He was trying to pin a mob killing on the man who ordered the contract. Now, everyone knows that simply isn't done. Once in a while the law can nab a button man, but they're afraid to go any higher. But this New York cop was dedicated. He learned who put out the contract and he went after him. Naturally, he had to be stopped. He wasn't afraid, because he hadn't learned yet the syndicate bosses are above the law. In fact, they control most of the law. So the cop had to be hit. And the mob brought in some clown named Coady to do the job. Only trouble was, Coady's intelligence level was approximately on a par with a ceramic ashtray. He thought of himself as a mad bomber. And he rigged a bomb in the cop's car. You remember what happened, don't you, Coady?"

Coady just looked at Straight. His eyes were numb.

"The cop and his wife had made love that morning. One of those wonderful mornings where you both feel drowsy as cats, and only after you hold each other for a while do you realize it's the perfect time for sex. That was the last time I ever made love, Coady, and it's not a bad memory to go out with. It was the last time because the morning lovemaking made the cop late for work. So while he was hurriedly getting dressed, his wife went into the garage to start the car for him. So it could warm up and he'd have a smooth drive."

Unconsciously, Coady cracked his knuckles.

"The explosion shook the entire house," Straight said. He was speaking in a deadly monotone. "Broke a few glasses in the kitchen. But it separated a warm, loving woman into small chunks of dead flesh. Oh, it was a fine bomb, Coady. It damaged the driver much more than the car. Does that give you a little more pride in your work?"

Coady coughed to clear his throat, then said hoarsely, "You've got the wrong man, Spinoza. I don't remember that cop's name for sure, but I'd know it if I heard it. It ain't Spinoza."

"Neither's mine," said Straight. "But the important thing is her name. Jill. Tell me, Coady, did you ever bother to learn the name of the woman you butchered? Did you know it was Jill? Did you even read the papers to find out her name was Jill? Jill Straight?"

"Straight," Coady mumbled.

"Spinoza's just an old philosopher friend of mine," said Straight. "I borrow his name on jobs because there are very few people who've ever heard of him. Makes it remarkably easy to check into hotels and rent cars. Much better than Jones or Smith. I'm Richard Straight, Coady."

Coady slumped in the chair. His eyes glazed. There was no questioning the conviction in Straight's voice.

"Tell me how it feels, Coady," Straight demanded. "Cranmer

won't see it coming. Jill certainly never anticipated a thing. And it's the anticipation that makes you squirm, isn't it?"

Coady couldn't speak. His sluggish mind was still struggling with the details of what was happening to him.

"Tell me how it feels, Coady," Straight said.

Then he pulled the trigger.

The roar of the .45 cascaded about the walls of the small motel room. Coady's chest blew apart, and his body and the chair crashed backward into the wall.

Straight said, "My God, Jill," and pointed the pistol back at the door to wait for Cranmer.

He was limping past the front of the Solano Inn when the white MG roared down the street and pulled up beside him. Cranmer's hand darted inside his coat, but then his mind regained control and told him the driver was no threat. He removed his hand from his jacket and watched the young man clamber out of the sports car.

"Mr. Cranmer," the man said, "my name's Donald Dorne. I'm a . . ."

"You're the newspaper reporter," Cranmer interrupted.

"Yes, sir, that's right. Listen, I'm sure you're busy, but you could make me a very happy man if you'd give me a few minutes of your time."

Cranmer scowled at him. He had been ready to call it a day and lie around the motel until Darden returned from Medwick. "You're right," he told the reporter. "I'm busy."

"Butch Maneri, your partner, told me to come see you," Dorne said, playing his trump.

Cranmer sighed. Always something coming up. If Butch had sent this character, it must mean he had some information. And the fact he knew Maneri was his partner intrigued Cranmer. "All right," he muttered. "But this had better be good."

Dorne winced imperceptibly.

"Let's go on back to my room," Cranmer said. "I could use a drink."

"Fine," said Dorne.

Dorne matched his pace to Cranmer's limp. As they neared room six they heard the sound of an explosion.

"What the hell?" said Dorne.

"Gunshot," Cranmer said tersely. "High caliber. You stay here."

Dorne stopped nervously in front of unit five. Cranmer walked to room six. He leaned against the wall beside the door and listened.

No sound.

Cranmer stood by the door listening for five minutes. Still no sound came from the motel room. He glanced back at Dorne and shrugged. No point in making an all-day affair of it. He extended his hand slowly and twisted the doorknob.

Even if he shoots, he'll only get the hand, Cranmer thought.

When the latch clicked free, Cranmer pushed the door inward. It slid open quietly, as if riding on a layer of fog. Cranmer remained on the outside, leaning almost casually on the wall beside the door.

After a long pause a voice from the interior of the motel room said, "Come on in, Steve. There's no gun on you."

Dorne started nervously when he heard the voice. Cranmer continued to lean against the wall, absently tracing patterns on the ground with his cane. He was trying to place the voice. It was a voice he had heard before, but not recently. The impression niggled at his mind that it was a voice from the past, a voice he had not heard for years. But Cranmer couldn't attach a person to the voice.

He hesitated, then made his decision and extracted his .32 from his shoulder holster. He motioned to the newspaper reporter to stay put. Then he raised the pistol and stepped quickly into the room.

A slender man in a black business suit sat on the bed in Cranmer's room. From the corner of his eye Cranmer saw the body on the floor near the far wall and recognized it as the result of the gunshot he had heard. The man on the bed had a pistol in his hand, but it was pointing at the floor. Cranmer continued to aim his gun at him.

"Hello, Steve," the man said casually.

Cranmer nodded slowly. "Hello, Dick. Long time."

Straight made a thin smile. "It's been a while," he agreed.

Cranmer kept the gun on him. "What's the story, Dick? What are you doing out of New York?"

Straight peered at him in mild astonishment, then laughed ironically. "You mean you don't know?" he asked.

Cranmer shrugged. "All I see is one live man and one dead man."

Straight said, "Then what the hell were you doing in the Gentry Hotel in Medwick Friday night?"

"Playing cards," Cranmer said, puzzled.

Straight laughed with genuine amusement. "I thought you had tracked us down," he said.

"Us?"

Straight indicated Coady's body. "You're working on the Taber kill, aren't you?"

Cranmer nodded.

"Well, you just solved it," Straight told him. He laughed again at the expression on Cranmer's face.

Cranmer said, "All right, I knew I was looking for two men. But what did you have to do with Taber?"

"Nothing," Straight said. "It was merely another job."

"A job," Cranmer mused. "Are you telling me you're a hit man?"

"That's what I'm telling you."

Cranmer shook his head. "Jesus Christ," he said. "What happened to the tough cop—the straight shooter?"

"He went sour," Straight said impassively. "A long time ago."

"Why'd you let me walk in here?"

Straight made the thin smile again. "I hired you to kill me. I'm making you a hit man."

Cranmer scowled at him. "What makes you think I'll kill you?" he demanded.

Straight shifted the Colt slightly in his hand. "Because I'll force you, Steve."

Cranmer shrugged. "Well, don't rush into anything," he said. "I know you, all right, but who's the guy on the floor?"

"Name's Hamilton Coady. He was another member of my esteemed profession."

"Why'd you shoot him?"

Straight shook his head. "That's another story. All you need to know is he killed Rope and Dreiser. He had strong hands."

"And Taber?"

"I hit Taber," Straight said calmly.

"With the straight razor?"

"With the razor."

"Damn," Cranmer said irritably. "You did go sour."

Straight shrugged.

"Hired killers," Cranmer pondered. "No wonder I couldn't make it fit together. I was working a crossword puzzle with no definitions. Who hired you, Dick?"

Straight shook his head.

"I need to know," Cranmer said.

"Can't help you," Straight said carelessly. "I'm not privy to such matters. From what I could gather while I was working up the hit, about half the town wanted Taber dead. Any one of them could have done the hiring."

Cranmer considered a moment, then said, "You were only hired to kill Taber, right? But Rope saw you at the Taber house, and you saw him. So you wasted him, too. Why kill Dreiser?"

"Habit," Straight said sardonically. "When I saw you at the hotel, I figured you were getting close, if you weren't already there. So I decided to follow you. This other clown was doing the same thing, and you weren't trying to avoid him. I didn't know why, but it gave us a good opportunity to follow you without stirring up suspicion. Coady killed him and then put some adhesive tape over his nose so he'd look like him."

"You killed a man just so you could follow me?"

"That's about it. And then, of course, it did mess you up with the law for a while. Confused the situation somewhat."

Cranmer shook his head disbelievingly.

Straight sighed. "I've had enough of this chatter, Steve. I'm going to raise this gun slowly. If you let me get it high enough, I'll kill you. One more won't make any difference to me."

"You know I'll do it," Cranmer told him.

"Sure. That's why I picked you."

Straight began to lift the Colt. Cranmer's expression didn't alter as he shot Straight precisely through the heart.

Straight fell back across the bed.

. . .

Donald Dorne had been listening outside the door. When he heard the second shot, he went into the room. He saw one dead man lying on the bed. He saw another corpse on the floor by the wall. When he looked at Coady's chest, he began to retch. He ran for the bathroom.

Cranmer joined him. "Try to keep it in the stool, kid," he said phlegmatically. He filled a glass with water and washed down two Demerols.

Then he got Jamie Darden on the phone.

"Hey, I was about to call you," Darden said. "I just now got back from Medwick, and you were right about . . ."

"Let it wait," Cranmer instructed. "There's a couple of corpses in my motel room. You might want to come take a look."

Cranmer gently replaced the receiver in the middle of Darden's spluttering.

Darden arrived at the Solano Inn with his siren screaming.

Dorne had left hurriedly, after recuperating from his attack of nausea. Cranmer had asked him why he had come to the motel, and Dorne said all he wanted was an interview. Cranmer chalked one up against Maneri. He told the newspaper reporter he now had a great eyewitness story and didn't need an interview. Dorne left, looking dazed and excited, probably with visions of the Pulitzer Prize in his mind, Cranmer thought.

Darden glared at the bodies in the room imperiously. "Well, Cranmer," he declared. "You've done it again."

Cranmer gave him an innocent look. "Look at the bright side, Darden. We obviated the necessity for a trial."

Darden looked at him blankly. "Meaning what?" he asked.

"Meaning these are our murderers," Cranmer said. "The fellow on the bed is the one who cut Taber's throat. His name's Dick Straight. Operates out of New York, or at least he used to. The one on the floor is his partner, name of Hamilton Coady. I don't know anything about him. Straight used to be a cop in New York City. Guess he decided there was more money on the other side of the law. And I suppose that's a solid assumption."

"What happened to them?" Darden asked.

Cranmer shrugged. "Don't know for sure. Straight shot Coady, but he wouldn't tell me why."

"Falling out among thieves," said Darden.

Cranmer coughed. "I shot Straight," he told the marshal. "Self-defense. That newspaper reporter, Dorne, was hanging around if you want a witness."

"What for?" Darden said. "I believe you. Guess I had better talk to Dorne for the official report, though. Do we just forget about the other now?"

"Hell, no," Cranmer said. "This was a pair of professional assassins, remember. They don't work on a whim, and they don't work cheap. Somebody hired them. Somebody who wanted Taber out of the way. And if I know anything about law, the man who hired them is as guilty as they are."

"If he ain't, he oughta be," Darden proclaimed. "Guess I better call the wagon."

The marshal made the call.

"Let's get over to the bank before they close," Cranmer said. "I want your official pull to get me a look at some records."

Darden, although puzzled, agreed. As soon as Dr. Keating arrived with an ambulance, Darden and Cranmer left for the bank.

Darden used the siren in his police car for the one-block trip to the bank. After a bit of persuasion the bank president allowed his records to be examined without a court order.

Then Cranmer called the county commissioners' office and found out where Maneri was working.

Maneri was digging a grave. He hadn't realized his crew was responsible for opening graves in the county cemeteries. Shoveling dirt, though, wasn't really any worse than struggling with asphalt as long as he could keep his mind away from the purpose of the digging.

McIntosh Johnson had appeared shortly after the noon break and picked three men to go into western Solano County and dig a grave. His eyes had glinted with perverse pleasure as he chose Maneri.

Maneri had learned enough about the deceased to satisfy him even if he had been interested. His two companions had discussed the dead man's entire family tree: who had married whom, who had died recently, who was prospering, who was preparing to die, who deserved to be dead although he was healthy.

The siren of Jamie Darden's car interrupted the colloquy. Darden parked at the edge of the small cemetery and picked his way through the graves as though he were walking on soft-boiled eggs. When he reached the group, he said, "Which one's Maneri?"

Maneri held up his hand like a schoolboy.

"You're wanted," the marshal said laconically. He turned and walked back to his car.

Maneri saw Cranmer sitting in the car. He told his companions, "Tell Johnson I've been arrested for sodomy," and followed Darden. He climbed into the back seat. "What's up?" he asked Cranmer.

"It's breaking," Cranmer told him. He recited a hurried account of the shootings at the motel and told Maneri what Darden had learned in Medwick and what the bank records had revealed.

"I figured you'd want to be in on the kill," Cranmer said. "Why in the hell did you send that newspaper reporter after me?"

Maneri grinned at him. "That's the price you pay for calling yourself the boss," he said. "I'm not authorized to make statements to the press."

"Terrific," Cranmer mumbled.

The eldritch wailing of Darden's siren made conversation difficult as they roared down a gravel road.

"Is there some particular reason to hurry that I'm unaware of?" Maneri asked Cranmer.

Cranmer made an eloquent gesture in Darden's direction and grinned.

Darden said, "Do you want to go . . . ?"

"Let's go get John Fairchild," said Cranmer.

John Fairchild, Solano's city manager, crossed his legs and peered apprehensively at the quartet surrounding him. He knew Jamie Darden and Peter Brindle, the mayor, of course, and he had met the man named Cranmer one time. He didn't know the young man with red hair.

They were in Peter Brindle's small workshop. The mayor was once again wearing blue overalls over a blue denim shirt. He had been working on a refrigerator and held a crescent wrench in his hand. He leaned insouciantly against the refrigerator and watched the proceedings.

Cranmer, Maneri and Darden stood in an irregular semicircle around Fairchild.

Cranmer did the talking. "I suppose you men have read in the papers that I'm not really an insurance investigator," he began.

Brindle and Fairchild nodded.

"I am an investigator, though," Cranmer said. "A private one. This man"—indicating Maneri—"is my assistant. We've been working on the Arthur Taber murder. At first we weren't even sure it wasn't a suicide. But Michael Rope's death pretty well settled that. Now, we learned Taber was a rather unpopular man. Even his wife didn't like him. But the person who hired us was convinced Taber's death had something to do with his refusal to sell his building to you folks so you could have a new courthouse."

Cranmer paused to light a cigarette. "Frankly," he continued, "I had a hard time buying that theory. Most murders are committed either for gain or in the heat of passion. This one was well set up, so that ruled out passion. Leaving gain. I couldn't see where anyone would gain that much by forcing Taber—or Taber's widow, actually—to sell the jewelry store. The architect interested me for a while. His business is hardly prospering, and a six percent commission on a construction project of two hundred thousand dollars would make a healthy boost in his income. Still, twelve thousand dollars didn't seem gain enough."

Fairchild crossed his legs the other way. He was sitting on a small wooden chair in the workshop. Brindle watched Cranmer with a politician's deadpan.

"It was common knowledge in Solano that Taber and his wife were playing around on each other. That's a possible motive for murder. But we've ruled out passion, remember? So I discounted the extramarital affairs. To tell you the truth, Rope was my favorite suspect until he called me and said he'd seen the murderers."

Cranmer hesitated a moment, then repeated: "Murderers. Plural. Now, I have to admit that threw me for a loop. Here I was searching for one killer, and I find out there are two. I couldn't fit two killers into any imaginable pattern. But that question cleared itself up this afternoon. The killers showed up at my place, planning to eliminate another nuisance. Unfortunately, their plans went awry, and I eliminated them instead. But I knew one of them. A hit man from New York City. In case you're unfamiliar with the term, a hit man is a professional killer. A man who renders services the same as any good businessman, with no questions asked. And they draw a pretty good stipend for their services, don't they, Brindle?"

The mayor's face remained immobile. "I wouldn't know, Mr. Cranmer," he said stoically. "You've lost me."

Cranmer shook his head mournfully. "I haven't lost nearly as much as you, Brindle. The marshal here went over to Medwick this morning and checked out your gambling losses. You blew a couple of thousand the night I was there; and you played like a man who needed to win. Seems like the more you need to win, the more you lose, doesn't it? Anyway, you've dropped a bundle. Gambling's illegal in this state, so the man who runs the poker game was more than glad to cooperate with Marshal Darden in return for being left alone. Then we checked your bank account this afternoon—after we learned it was a hired killing. You drew five thousand dollars from your savings account only a week before Taber was hit. Is five thousand the going price now?"

Brindle remained unshaken. "Like you said, I've been losing at poker. I withdrew the money to help cover the losses."

"Good recovery," Cranmer said. "You see, Brindle, my whole trouble was I was looking at the courthouse project and the federal grant backwards. I was looking for someone who stood to gain if the courthouse was built. What I should have been looking for was someone who would suffer if the grant had to be returned. Fairchild?"

The city manager twitched in his chair. His eyes darted nervously from face to face.

"You've probably been wondering why you're here," Cranmer said. "It's simple, really. I need the answer to one question: who had control of the grant from the government?"

Fairchild's throat was clogged and he coughed to clear it. He glanced guiltily at Peter Brindle. "Pete handled it," he said finally. "Small town like this, people double up on duties. The mayor always acts as treasurer."

"That's what I figured," Cranmer said, pleased. "Would you care to place a wager on how much of that grant money is left?"

Fairchild looked down at the floor.

"You had to act fast, Brindle," Cranmer said. "People were talking about giving all that money back. As I recall a newspaper story I read about it, there was going to be a special meeting of some sort to decide. But you didn't have the money to return, did you? You blew it over a card table in Medwick. And that trip to Reno you made three weeks ago probably didn't help much either. Oh, yes, we know about that too, Brindle."

Brindle's eyes turned frantic. He stood up straight by the refrigerator. Darden moved closer to him.

Cranmer snapped his fingers. "Oh, I almost forgot something," he said casually. "The hit man from New York City didn't die immediately. And he didn't have anything else to lose, so he told us who hired him. He gave us your name, Brindle."

Brindle's shoulders slumped, then he took a quick step and smashed Jamie Darden across the temple with the crescent wrench he had been holding throughout Cranmer's performance.

Darden reeled across the floor and stumbled into Maneri. Before Maneri could extricate himself, Brindle darted out the back door of the workshop.

Fairchild sat catatonically in the wooden chair.

Cranmer limped to the back door in time to see Brindle leap into a dirty white pickup. The engine fired immediately, and Brindle raced the car down the alley that ran behind the shop.

Maneri joined Cranmer at the back door. "Come on!" he said. "We'll get him in Darden's heap."

Maneri ran through the shop, and Cranmer hobbled after him as fast as he could. Darden rolled into a sitting position and moaned, holding his head. Cranmer stepped around him. "God damn you," he snarled. "I hope they amputate."

Maneri had the police car's engine revved up by the time Cranmer reached it. Cranmer tossed his cane into the back seat and climbed in. After a moment he said, "What the hell are you waiting for? A sign from heaven?"

Maneri grinned but kept his eyes on the street. "That alley back there doesn't come out anywhere but on this street," he told Cranmer. "He can't cut back the other way. It's just a question of which way he turns when he comes out."

"Goddamn geography major," Cranmer muttered. "Can you believe that goddamn cowboy, letting Brindle take him like that? And where in the hell were you?"

"Well, you're the boss," Maneri said. "I figured it was your place to be the hero. Here he comes!"

The white pickup took the corner on two wheels and headed out of town in the direction opposite that which the police car was facing. Maneri made an abrupt U turn, adding to Solano County's rubber bill, and pursued the pickup.

"Too bad I haven't got the Fiat," Maneri said. "It's got quite a bit more juice than this wreck."

"This is bound to outrun a pickup truck," Cranmer said. "Can't you turn off that damn siren?"

"In case you haven't noticed, I'm trying to steer this beast," Maneri said. "You should be able to find the switch."

After a brief search, Cranmer managed to still the siren.

"We're gaining ground," Maneri said.

The brake lights on the pickup flashed, and it careened off the highway onto a county road. Maneri slid through the turn with a wide smile on his face. "That cat doesn't know I built the roads in this county," he said. "He hasn't got a chance."

But the road was often broken by curves, and Maneri was having little success catching the pickup. "Why don't you shoot his tires?" he asked Cranmer seriously. "This could last a week."

"I need the son of a bitch alive," Cranmer said. "There's a loose end or two left."

"Hell, he'll be alive," said Maneri. "A deadly shot like you shouldn't mistake a driver for a tire."

"Just catch him," Cranmer ordered.

Maneri narrowed the gap as they hit a straight stretch of road. Brindle put the pickup in the middle of the road, so Maneri couldn't pull up alongside.

"Well, boss, how do you suggest we stop him?" Maneri asked. "You'll never have a better shot."

"Run the son of a bitch off the road," Cranmer said.

Maneri glanced at him quickly.

"Let's tear up that goddamn cowboy's car," Cranmer said.

"The one in front of us or the one we're in?"

"Both."

Maneri shrugged slightly. A curve in the road was approaching. As Brindle swung wide to navigate the turn, Maneri stomped the accelerator and moved inside the pickup. He kept the police car going straight, and Brindle couldn't make the turn.

The police car collided with the pickup, forcing it off the road at the same moment Cranmer yelled, "Not here!"

But it was too late.

The pickup tumbled into a deep ravine, overturned twice and crashed into a tree.

Maneri battled the police car to a stop, just at the edge of the road. "Jesus," he said.

"Goddamnit," Cranmer said quietly. "I'll give you five to two the son of a bitch is dead."

Brindle was.

Eight

Denise Taber swung her front door open and glared at Cranmer. Then she saw Maneri, and bafflement replaced irritation on her face.

"Aren't you ever going to leave?" she said sourly to Cranmer.

"We found out what happened to your husband," Cranmer said politely. "Thought you might be interested."

She opened the door wider and they followed her into the house. When they were seated, she looked at Maneri and said, "Don't tell me you're involved in this?"

"I work with Cranmer," said Maneri.

"Well, I'll be damned," said Denise Taber. "Everyone's a cop."

"At least you made a month's rent off me," Maneri said.

She turned her gaze to Cranmer. "You said you found out about Art. What?"

"Peter Brindle had him killed," Cranmer said carelessly. "He'd been milking that EDA grant and was afraid he'd have to make good on it if Taber wouldn't sell the store. He figured you'd sell, so he got rid of your husband."

Denise looked at him skeptically. "I don't believe it," she said firmly. "I know Pete Brindle. He couldn't kill anyone."

"Maybe not personally," Cranmer said. "But he had the money to hire it done. Oh, there's no doubt about it, Mrs. Taber. We braced him with the evidence, and he panicked and ran. In a sense, you could say he committed suicide."

"He's dead!"

"Ran his car, truck, off the road and crushed himself. But he told us something before he made his break, something that cleared up a point that had been bothering me. You see, Brindle was only a small-town mayor. Had a reputation to protect, and I suppose he was desperate to protect it. But your husband was murdered by hired killers, Mrs. Taber. Hired assassins."

Cranmer lit a Camel and thoughtfully blew smoke at the ceiling. Then he continued: "After we learned professional killers were involved, the series of murders began to make sense. And I was already leery of Brindle. I'd seen him lose more money in a card game than a man in his position should have lost. And his reaction was what interested me most; he was really sick. But there was one sticking point—until Brindle came clean."

Cranmer sucked on his cigarette and waited. He won the battle of nerves. Denise Taber asked, "All right, Mr. Cranmer, what was your sticking point?"

Cranmer exhaled and pointed his burning cigarette at Denise. "They don't list assassins in the yellow pages, Mrs. Taber. It takes contacts in some pretty strange places to locate them. Now, I didn't see any way for Brindle, a small-town mayor, to have those contacts. But your husband had them, didn't he, Mrs. Taber? A fence for stolen jewelry would have a sizable list of contacts: customers, people to go to in case of trouble. People big enough to keep the law off his back. And an address book would be a perfect place to keep a list of contacts, wouldn't it? And it would be sensitive enough to keep locked up. Face it, Mrs. Taber, what your husband had, you had. That's why you destroyed the address book. Brindle told us you gave him the name of the man to call."

Cranmer stubbed out the Camel. He'd run one successful bluff today: telling Brindle that Straight had named him. He waited to see if he could be lucky twice.

Denise Taber hesitated a moment, considering. She rubbed two long tapered fingernails together. The slight scratching was the only sound in the room. Then Denise let her jaw drop, and her face assumed a horrified expression. "Oh, my God," she said dramatically. "I killed my husband. I did give Peter the name."

Cranmer relaxed back into his chair.

But Denise continued: "He tricked me, the bastard. He told me he was in trouble, that someone was threatening his life. He knew about Art's past, and he asked me for help. He said he couldn't ask Art because of the trouble they were having over the courthouse project. So I gave him the name. Then I got frightened and burned the address book." She put her head in her hands.

Cranmer looked at Maneri, made a face and shrugged. It would be hard to disprove. He lit another Camel in disgust. "Didn't you get suspicious when your husband died?" he asked.

"Why, no," said Denise Taber. "I thought Art committed suicide. Everyone did until you came along."

"Yeah, well, sorry about that," Cranmer said ironically. "Let's go, Butch."

Denise accompanied them to the door. "I'll have to live with this the rest of my life," she said.

Then she smiled.

Jamie Darden's only comment when he heard about Brindle was: "Well, Cranmer, like you said, it osculates the necessity for a trial."

Tracy Zantell gave Maneri a glass of milk, and he used it to wash down medicine.

"That's about all of it," he said. "The damn thing got out of hand. I guess that's the trouble with button men: they kill their way into trouble, then they try to kill their way out of it. They had absolutely no reason for killing that simple-minded insurance investigator. To them, it was simply a matter of convenience."

Tracy nodded. "I suppose I can see why they killed Mike. But goddamnit, why did Brindle have to kill Art? Or hire him killed? Is a man's reputation worth a life?"

It was a rhetorical question. Maneri decided to let it go. He could have mentioned that Art Taber's reputation had been worth $1,000 a month to him, but he let it go. However, the notion prompted a question: "Say, Auntie, how are you going to make it without the grand a month from Taber?"

"Oh, I'll survive. My gift shop actually makes a little profit, and I've got some money set back."

"Don't forget our fee," Maneri reminded her. "It'll be high—especially since Steve was stuck with a black-and-white TV." His eyes twinkled. "And you can't buy me off in trade."

Tracy smiled. It was her first honest smile since Maneri had arrived. "Send the bill," she said. "I said it would be worth paying. At least they didn't get away with it. What bothers me is, if I hadn't hired you, three people would still be alive."

"You're not counting the hit men?"

"Believe me, dear nephew, I consider their loss the world's gain."

Maneri shook his head. "I wish I knew the whole story. Steve said Straight used to be a damn good cop in New York City. Well, you never learn everything."

"And that's probably best," said Tracy. She paused a moment and looked at Maneri searchingly. "Butch, I want you to tell me something honestly. I don't plan to do anything about it, but it's something I need to know: Do you believe what Denise said about why she gave Brindle the name?"

"Yep," Maneri lied casually, without hesitation. "If you'd seen the expression on her face, you wouldn't have to ask."

"All right," Tracy said. "Thanks."

Maneri stood up. "Gotta hit the road," he said.

Tracy smiled. "Sure you can't stay and improve my spirits?"

"Lady, there's nothing I'd like better. But Cranmer's a hard man. He's waiting for me at the motel, and he says we've got time to get home before the football game starts. And you know Cranmer and ball games."

He walked to the front door. "Oh, Tracy, one good thing. Nobody ever found out who hired us."

Tracy shrugged. "It doesn't really matter, does it?"

"Everything matters," Maneri said.

Epilogue

August McEachern accepted a banana daiquiri from Harold, sipped it delicately and nodded approval.

"The Oklahoma affair is rounding out nicely," McEachern said. "I sent Rimson to the Bahamas for a while, as a precaution, but I don't believe that disappoints him too greatly. We lost Coady, but that's somewhat like losing a migraine headache."

"Yes, sir, Mr. McEachern," said Harold.

McEachern sighed. "You just can't trust people any more, Harold. It's ironic, I suppose, that Straight didn't turn me over. I guess I needn't have worried about him. But I almost wish he'd justified my fears. It's annoying to think I misjudged him so badly. It's a quandary."

"Yes, sir, Mr. McEachern," said Harold.

"One thing, Harold: let's build a dossier on this Steven Cranmer. I don't favor retaliation: that's childish. But he might make a good man for us. Who do we have in Oklahoma City?"

"Sandusky, sir. He's small time, but he should be able to provide us with the data."

"Very good, Harold. Turn him loose."

"Yes, sir, Mr. McEachern," said Harold.

Cranmer was sleeping on the avocado couch in his office when Maneri entered. He opened his eyes groggily. "Not again," he complained.

Maneri fingered the beard which was becoming established on

his face. The beard hadn't filled in yet, and Maneri's face looked as if it were covered with red blisters.

"I got to missing it," Maneri explained. "And the kind of luck I've been having with women lately, I figured I needed to change something. Anything perking?"

Cranmer laughed. "Are you kidding? We made enough out of the Solano mess to keep us in booze and blondes for a while. And I don't mean rotgut and floozies. I only hope my energy outlasts the money."

"What energy is that?"

"I turned down three cases this morning."

Maneri shook his head. "You lack ambition, Steve. I need some work to supplement my pool income."

"With most people it'd be the other way around," Cranmer commented. He hoisted himself from the couch and limped into the bathroom. He emerged with an empty medicine bottle. "If you truly crave manual labor," he told Maneri, "go fetch me some Demerol."

"Always here to serve," Maneri said sarcastically. But he took the empty bottle and left the office.

Cranmer splashed bourbon into his coffee cup.

Cindy Dawson entered and spoke languidly. "Your cardplaying friend's here," she announced. "Sandusky? Says he's still being gypped. Shall I bring him in?"

"Chase him. Tell him we're overworked and understaffed. Tell him anything, but get him out of here. I haven't recuperated from the last job yet."

"Do you plan to?" she asked archly. She returned to the outer office to dispose of the potential client.

Cranmer swallowed bourbon and coffee, leaned back in the chair behind his desk and closed his eyes. He hadn't had a nightmare for a week. And Tracy Zantell had paid her outrageous bill with a check that didn't bounce. She didn't even balk at Cranmer's taxi bill for the trip to Medwick for poker.

Half an hour later Maneri returned. Cranmer was sleeping in his chair, his legs propped on the desk. Maneri kicked the table and Cranmer's eyes opened slowly. "You're worse than an alarm clock," he complained.

Maneri grinned at him. “And you’re an angel of mercy,” he said. He set the bottle of Demerol on the desk.

Cranmer peered at the bottle suspiciously. “Angel of mercy? Have you been raiding my pills?”

“Never, dad. You know I’m straight. But you wouldn’t believe the beautiful pharmacist I met. The beautiful *single* pharmacist I met.”

“I trust it’s a woman,” Cranmer said sourly.

“Is she ever. She also happens to be free tonight.”

Cranmer wagged his head sadly. “I predict your gastritis will flare up again.”

“Yeah,” Maneri grinned. “But watch me arrange a discount on my medicine.”

About the Author

STEVE KNICKMEYER was born in Cassville, Missouri, in 1944. He graduated with a degree in history from the University of Oklahoma, Phi Beta Kappa, in 1967. He now lives in Ada, Oklahoma, where he divides his time among journalism, literary criticism and writing fiction. He is married and has three sons. *Straight* is his first novel.